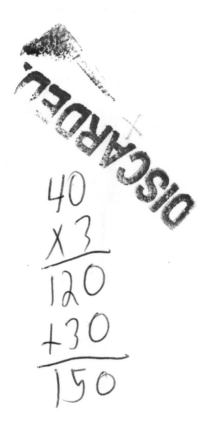

$$
\begin{array}{r}
40 \\
\times 3 \\
\hline
120 \\
+30 \\
\hline
150
\end{array}
$$

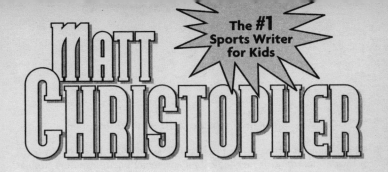

The #1 Sports Writer for Kids

RETURN OF THE
HOME RUN KID

Little, Brown and Company
Boston   New York   London

First Paperback Edition

The characters and events portrayed in this book are fictitious. Any sim-
ilarity to real persons, living or dead, is coincidental and not intended by
the author.

Library of Congress Cataloging-in-Publication Data

Christopher, Matt.
    Return of the home run kid / by Matt Christopher. — 1st ed.
      p.   cm.
    Summary: Sylvester Coddmyer III is having a dismal baseball
season until he takes advice from a mysterious ex-ballplayer
named Cheeko and starts to play more aggressively.
    ISBN 0-316-14273-5 (pb)
    [1. Baseball — Fiction.]   1. Title
PZ7.C458Rf 1992
[Fic] — dc20   91-30817

PB: 10 9 8 7

COM-MO

Printed in the United States of America

RETURN OF THE
HOME RUN KID

Crack!

Sylvester Coddmyer III dropped the bat and stared deep into the outfield. The ball soared over the center fielder's outstretched glove. It was heading toward the fence. It was going over. It was going . . . going . . .

"Wake up, Sylvester!" Coach Stan Corbin's raw voice cut through the cool spring air. "Did you come here to play baseball or nap?"

Pulling his cap over his thatch of blond hair, Sylvester blinked and jumped up. He'd been dozing at the far end of the bench. The dugout was so warm, and he really hadn't expected to hear his name called. After all, he hardly ever got to play these days.

It was such a nice dream, too. It reminded him of last season when he was the Hooper Redbirds'

1

leading hitter. Back then it seemed as if he could hit nothing but home runs — except for the last game. He had struck out twice before getting a double, but that drove in what turned out to be the winning runs. That amazing season had earned Sylvester a trophy for being the best athlete in the history of Hooper Junior High.

To this day, he felt it was all due to Mr. Baruth. Sylvester wasn't even good enough to be considered a so-so player until that mysterious stranger showed up and started giving him pointers.

But Mr. Baruth had left town almost as suddenly as he had appeared. This season there was no outside help. At first Sylvester had figured he didn't need any. He thought he'd just show up and start belting the ball without a lot of effort or a lot of practice. It hadn't happened that way. Coasting along just didn't work, and his game had turned dismal. The coach really had no reason to let him play.

Now it was the top of the fourth inning, the score 3–0 in the Seneca Indians' favor, and the coach had decided that Bobby Kent, the Redbirds' star outfielder, needed a rest.

"Grab your glove, Sylvester, and take Bobby's

place out in center. Bobby, you've done well, kid. Take a break," said the coach.

The Redbirds' tall center fielder looked surprised. He glanced over at the short and stocky Sylvester and smirked as he flopped down on the bench.

Thanks for the vote of confidence, Bobby, Sylvester thought with a scowl. Just because you're hot out there now. . . . Well, I can tell you it doesn't always last.

Glove in hand, Sylvester ran out of the dugout and nearly tripped on his straggling shoelaces. He'd loosened them when he felt his feet getting cramped from dangling off the bench. Quickly tying them, he ran off toward his playing position.

"Hi, Syl!" yelled Ted Sobel from his position in left field. Dressed in his Redbird red uniform with white trim, Ted looked neat and bright, like a Christmas ornament.

"Hi!" replied Sylvester. It felt good to be out on the field with the sun shining down on him. It was a little bit like last year when, following Mr. Baruth's coaching tips, he'd made a series of fantastic catches on top of his great hitting. Maybe the coach and his teammates remembered how well he had played, after all.

3

"Hey, Syl," Les Kendall, the right fielder, greeted him offhandedly.

Les was the team's second leading hitter — right after that new kid, Trent Sturgis, who played short-stop. Trent did a good job fielding, but it was his hitting streak that made him the focus of everyone's attention.

As Syl mentally compared Trent's playing abilities to his own, his confidence sagged. He forgot all about Mr. Baruth and silently wished that any balls hit to the outfield would go to either left or right field.

The infield chatter rattled on as the Indians' catcher, Scott Corrigan, stepped into the batter's box. Wearing a black-trimmed yellow uniform, Scott was the Indians' cleanup hitter. So far he'd gotten a two-bagger.

Scott took two balls and a strike, then laced one deep to left.

"Back! Back!" Sylvester yelled to Ted as the ball rose in a high arc over the field.

Ted raced back as far as he could go, then watched as the ball soared over his head and disappeared behind the fence.

As he turned and watched Scott trot around the

4

bases, Sylvester groaned. No need to hurry, he thought. I know just how he feels. A pang of envy pinched somewhere deep in his chest.

Rooster Adams was up next and slammed a low, clothesline drive straight out to center field. Sylvester's heart leapt into his throat as he saw the ball coming directly at him.

Mr. Baruth sprang into his mind. Remember what he told you. Keep your eye right on that ball and get under it. Sylvester ran forward, his arm stretched out in front of him.

Splat! The ball smacked into the pocket of his glove. And then it vanished.

He searched the green turf around his feet, thinking that he had dropped it.

"Your glove! Your glove, Syl!" Ted yelled at him from over in left field.

Sylvester looked at his glove and his heart uncoiled like an overwound spring. There, nesting in the center of the well-oiled glove, was the red-and-blue-threaded white ball.

He breathed a sigh of relief, picked out the ball, and tossed it to Jim Cowley, the Redbirds' second baseman.

"Good catch, Syl!" Jim called to him.

Syl's smile faded. Was Jim surprised he'd made a good catch or was he saying that to be nice?

He wondered whether Joyce Dancer was in the stands and what she thought of his catch. Joyce was twelve, a year younger than Sylvester, but they spent a lot of time with each other. They'd just started going to movies together.

There was no time to think about that. He had to pay attention to the game.

Stan Falls, up next, rapped out a single over shortstop. Then Jon Buckley struck out. Terry Barnes, the Redbirds' pitcher, was erratic today, first hot, then cold. Sylvester remembered the two batters he'd fanned in the first inning as well as the three runs he'd given up to the Indians in the second.

"C'mon, Terry! Strike 'em out!" Sylvester yelled as the Indians' shortstop, Dick Wasser, stepped into the box.

Dick hugged the plate as if he were defending it. He let two of Terry's pitches go by for strikes, then took a walk as Terry flubbed the next four.

Two out, two on as the Indians' pitcher, Burk Riley, came to bat.

"Easy out!" Sylvester yelled. "Easy out!" Burk's bat had hardly touched the ball so far today.

Burk took a called strike, then laced Terry's next pitch to right center field. Both Sylvester and Les Kendall raced toward the ball. Les got there first, scooped it up, and heaved it to third base. But his throw was short. Dick Wasser held up on third. Stan Falls raced in to score.

Bus Riley, the Indians' leadoff batter, then flied out to left to end the inning.

Seneca Indians 5, Hooper Redbirds 0.

Sylvester ran off the field, glad that the half inning was over without any disasters on his part. He had made a good catch, but what if he had missed it? What would happen next time a ball came at him like that? Would he remember what he'd learned from Mr. Baruth again? All these thoughts seemed to bounce around in his head at the same time, making him nervous.

"Grab a bat, Sylvester!" the red-haired, freckle-faced scorekeeper Billy Haywood called to him as he came trotting off the field. "Start it off with a big one, pal!"

Start it off? Sylvester hadn't realized he'd be up at

bat so soon. This made him even more nervous than he'd been in the field.

Sylvester took a couple of deep breaths, hoping that would help calm him down.

He yanked his maroon batting gloves out of his pocket, slipped them on, selected a bat — a brown one with white tape around the handle — put on a helmet, and strode to the plate.

Heart racing, he scraped the dirt with his shoes, pretending to get a better grip by digging them in. Time, just a little more time. That's all he needed. Time for his heartbeat to slow down.

Burk steamed in two pitches, a ball and a strike. Then came another pitch that looked as good as any Sylvester could hope for.

Clunk! Bat barely connected with ball, and the ball rolled away from the plate like a frightened worm.

Sylvester dropped his bat and raced for first base, knowing all the while that his short legs would never beat the throw. It was a sure out. He could practically hear the call.

Suddenly, there was a yell from the crowd, and he saw the ball fly over the first baseman's head. It was a rotten throw! What a break!

He touched first and ran on to second, where he stayed, listening to applause from the Redbirds' supporters and boos from the Indians'.

"Hey, Codfish," yelled one of the Indians' fans. "You know what? You're just lucky!"

That stung, but Sylvester tried to brush it off. Sticks and stones, he thought. Mr. Baruth had pointed out that there were characters like that in every crowd — and that you just had to ignore them. Instead, he tried to concentrate on the next batter.

Duane Francis, the Redbirds' sandy-haired third baseman and Sylvester's closest friend on the team, took the first pitch — a strike — then rapped the next one between center and left field for a double, to score his pal.

"Nice going, Syl," second baseman Jim Cowley called as he came into the dugout.

Nobody else said anything. They hardly looked at him. It even seemed as though Trent Sturgis, bat in hand, deliberately turned away as Sylvester walked by him.

"Okay, bring him in, Eddie!" shouted Coach Corbin, standing and clapping in the third base coaching box.

Catcher Eddie Exton didn't. He fanned out. Terry, up next, bounced a one-hopper to the pitcher for the second out. Sylvester groaned with his teammates as they saw one of their best hitters go down.

It was now Jim Cowley's turn at bat.

"Out of the lot, Jim!" Sylvester yelled.

Jim's hit off the first pitch didn't go out of the lot, but it was good enough for a single, scoring Duane.

That was the last hit of the inning. Seneca Indians 5, Hooper Redbirds 2.

Terry and the Redbirds' defense held the Indians in check in the top of the fifth. In the bottom of the inning, with Les on first, thanks to a walk, and Trent on first by virtue of a clean single to short right field, the first baseman, Jerry Ash, flied out. That brought Sylvester up to the plate.

"Okay, Syl!" yelled the coach. "Let's see you clean the bases!"

Sylvester swung at Burk's first three pitches. He missed every one of them.

2

Booooo!" yelled the same Indians' fan who'd called him names before. "You know what? You really stink! Like a dead codfish!"

Sylvester knew better, but the words still stung. As he headed for the dugout, he felt like a total failure. Of all the dumb times to strike out, he thought.

It wasn't like this last year, he reminded himself. He would have gotten a three-run homer if he was hitting like back then. That would have shut up that wise guy!

Yeah, but that was then. This is now. He couldn't avoid reminding himself of that, too.

"No sweat," said his pal Duane, as he passed Sylvester on his way to the plate. "You'll get 'em next time."

Sure, thought Sylvester sourly. Next time.

11

Duane singled to keep things alive, but then Eddie Exton struck out.

Indians 5, Redbirds 3.

Stan Falls, leading off for the Indians in the top of the sixth and last inning, hit a three-two pitch to deep center field. As it came at him, Sylvester wished that it would be deep enough to sail over the fence.

It wasn't. Still, he only had to back up a few steps and it would be his.

But the ball hit the tip of his glove, not its pocket, and glanced off onto the ground.

"Oh, no!" he groaned, as he sprang forward, retrieved the ball, and pegged it in to second base to hold the runner at first.

He could almost hear that obnoxious Indians' fan yelling at him in the midst of all the shouting from the stands.

Jon Buckley grounded out, and Dick Wasser flied out to right field. That brought up Burk Riley, the Indians' pitcher. It should have been an easy out, but Burk walked.

Two men on, two out, and Bus Riley, Burk's brother, came up next.

Crack! He lambasted Terry's first pitch directly at Trent, who caught it for the third out.

It was the Redbirds' final opportunity to win the game. As Sylvester joined his teammates in the dugout, Bobby Kent snorted.

"I don't know why the coach put you in, Coddmyer," Bobby said. "Maybe you were a hotshot last year, but you're nothin' but a cold turkey now."

Sylvester's face turned beet red.

"I didn't ask him to," he mumbled. "It was his own idea."

Trent, who was sitting nearby, cut in smugly. "Maybe he feels he has to, just because you're wearing a uniform." The tall shortstop had already acquired quite a reputation as an up-and-coming ballplayer with a batting average of over .400. Add to this a really good throwing arm and the result was an inflated ego.

Sylvester's heart sank. After all, he thought, just because I love to play doesn't mean I'm any good for the team. I *was* great last year, but where does that put me now?

"Here we go, Terry!" The sound of Coach Corbin encouraging Terry Barnes called Syl back to the present. Terry gave it his best as he led off with a single between third base and shortstop. Syl joined in the cheers. He figured maybe if the Redbirds pulled it out in the end, the fans would forget about his stupid fielding error. Even his freak hit had been stupid. It was just by luck that he'd gotten on base.

"Way to go!" Coach Corbin called from the third base coaching box. "Okay, Jim! Let's keep it going!"

But Jim flied out, and so did Ted. Then Trent Sturgis stepped into the batter's box.

"C'mon, Trent!" Sylvester yelled, forgetting for a moment how Trent had snubbed him. Right now, all he wanted was for the Redbirds to win.

Trent walked.

The Redbirds were still alive!

"Atta boy, Trent!" Sylvester cheered along with the fans in the stands. "Let's keep it rolling, Les!"

Les didn't. He hit a pitch sky-high to the third baseman, and the Indians took the game, 5–3.

As the disappointed team left the dugout, Sylvester kept his cap pulled low over his forehead.

"Syl! Sylvester Coddmyer!"

Syl recognized the high-pitched voice calling to

14

him. He got a little flustered when he turned and saw Joyce Dancer running toward him from the bleachers.

"Syl . . . oh, Syl!" he heard Bobby chant in a mocking, girlish voice, tickling Trent's funny bone as they drifted off in gales of laughter.

But the two wise guys made no impression on the young girl. Her deeply tanned arms, a result of long sessions on the tennis court, were wrapped around a healthy stack of books.

"Hi, Syl," she said, as she got closer to him. "Some game, huh?"

"Yeah," he mumbled, his voice barely audible.

He slowed his pace to make sure they wouldn't catch up with Bobby and Trent. It was no secret that he and Joyce were friends. But he didn't want to have to deal with those guys.

"Cheer up," Joyce said, breaking out in a big smile. "So you lost a ball game, not a war."

"To me it is a war," Sylvester grumbled.

"That's really nuts. But I know how you feel," Joyce said.

"You think so?"

"Sure I think so. I play tennis, remember? I've lost my share of matches. You don't think I like losing, do you?"

"'Course not. But you always look good, whether you win or lose," Sylvester said. Then he realized his words could be taken more than one way.

Joyce chuckled, hiking up the books in her arms. "Thanks, but I don't always feel good. I'm human, too!"

By now, they'd come to the end of a block.

"But you don't think that it's just like a war?" he asked.

"Nope." She laughed. "Not even a military conflict."

He finally laughed, too. "I guess you're right," he said. "It's just hard. I mean, I want to be good — at least some of the time — but it never happens lately."

"Yeah, being in a slump is the pits," she said. "Hey, you just have to do the best you can to get out of it. It's the only way it's going to happen."

"Thank you very much for your prescription, Dr. Dancer," he joked, a big grin on his face.

In fact, Joyce's cheerful nature was a little like

medicine to him. He felt like taking her hand and squeezing it gently. Sometimes they held hands at the movies. But he wouldn't dare do that here, out in the open. He could imagine how the other guys would howl and jeer if they saw.

Still, it was nice and comfortable, just walking down the street with her. Without even asking, he leaned over and took some of her books as they chattered away in the late afternoon. There was more and more shade these days as the leaves on the trees along the sidewalk grew greener and greener with the approach of summer.

Sylvester felt something else inside — hunger. His stomach was reminding him that he needed some nourishment. But that didn't stop him from enjoying his time with Joyce. He wished she lived five more blocks away instead of only two.

At last they were in front of her home, a white clapboard two-story house with shrubs and flowering bushes hugging its base.

Joyce took back her books and gave him what he liked to think was their secret wink.

"See you tomorrow," she said, then turned down the driveway toward the back door.

"Right," he said, winking back. "See you."

Still cozy and warm from the special feeling Joyce always seemed to impart, Sylvester walked slowly down the block and was about to cross over when a deep voice interrupted his thoughts.

"Sylvester! Sylvester Coddmyer the Third!"

For one split second, he flashed back to a year ago, to the moment when Mr. Baruth entered his life. But no, even though this was a man's voice, it wasn't the same.

He turned around, his forehead creased with curiosity as he stared at the man walking toward him. The man was tall and lanky, had a stubble of a beard, and wore a white sweatshirt and a hat with an old-fashioned letter *C* on it. No, this was definitely not Mr. Baruth.

"Got a minute, Sylvester?" the man asked.

Sylvester was sure he'd never seen this man before. He wondered how he knew his name.

"Well, sort of," he answered. He was glad they were in a friendly neighborhood, not far from his home — just in case this guy turned out to be some kind of weirdo.

But the stranger had a really nice smile as he

18

came forward and stretched out his right hand. Sylvester shook it cautiously, gazing into the man's dark eyes while he ran through his memory bank. Definitely, no one he'd ever seen before.

"Name's Cheeko," the man said. "Saw you play today. Whew! I hate to say it, but you sure have a lot of room for improvement, haven't you?"

He said it with a smile about a foot wide. Sylvester couldn't help but smile, too.

"You're right." He nodded.

"I bet you'd like to fill up that room and be a better ballplayer, right?"

"Right." The word had barely left Sylvester's lips when he suddenly recalled a conversation just like this with Mr. Baruth the first time they met.

"All right, then, listen to me," said the man named Cheeko. "I think I can help."

3

The man's words raced on, fast and punchy, nothing like the mellow, steady sound of Mr. Baruth's voice.

"I know about that home run streak you were on last year. Great. But you missed one thing, one thing the guy who coached you left out. You have to be a lot tougher, more aggressive. You wanna be a winner in this world, you've got to make a few moves, take a few shortcuts, too. You've got to stand up for what's yours and let 'em know you're not some kind of bug that anyone can step on. Get what I mean?"

As Sylvester drank in every word, he wondered how this man, a perfect stranger, knew so much about him. Especially, he couldn't figure out how "Cheeko" knew about his hot streak last year. And Mr. Baruth's coaching.

20

"Wait a minute," he asked. "Do you know Mr. Baruth? Are you a friend of his?"

"Baruth?" Cheeko's eyes crinkled up at the corners as he flashed his big smile again. "Sure I do. It's like we're old buddies. Matter of fact, that's how I heard about you."

"He told you about me?" Sylvester relaxed a little as soon as he heard that Cheeko was a friend of Mr. Baruth's. That automatically made him a better than average guy in Sylvester's book.

"Exactly!" said Cheeko. "That's why I dropped by to see how you were doing. Not great, huh? Nothing to brag about, right?"

"Right," Sylvester admitted, looking down at the toe of his right shoe as he kicked at a pebble.

"Hey, I know you can do better," Cheeko went on. Despite his strong, almost pushy way of talking, Sylvester was interested in what he had to say.

Sylvester scowled. "Well, I sure would like to get out of this darn slump."

"You can," Cheeko insisted. "Hey, let me work out with you a little. Believe me, I can show you a few things the other guys on the field wouldn't ever even think of. Tell you what, I'll bring the baseballs. All

21

you need to bring is a bat and your glove. Whaddya say? You up for it?"

A million questions raced through Sylvester's mind but he could only drag out a few.

"I . . . I want to be a better player," he said, "but how come you want to work out with me? Why not some other kid?"

"Hey, I told you, Mr. Baruth said you were an okay guy," Cheeko said, still smiling. "I hate to see anybody get a raw deal. There're still a lot of scores to settle."

Sylvester wasn't sure what he meant, but his heart was pounding at thoughts of his winning streak coming back to him.

"You sure you have the time to spend with me? Don't you have to work?" he asked.

Cheeko chuckled. "Time's the one thing I have. Plenty of it. You might say I'm sort of retired. So what's the word? Game?"

The vision of the blaze of glory that he felt every time the ball soared over the fence, every time he made an almost impossible catch, every time he crossed the plate at a steady trot, exploded in his mind. Sylvester would give almost anything to bring back those moments. There was no room in his mind for doubts now.

"Game!" he answered.

"Great!" said Cheeko. "See you after supper."

He put out a hand and Sylvester almost leapt to give him a high five.

As Cheeko headed off in the other direction, Sylvester started to run down the street toward his home. He hadn't gotten far when he realized he had a big step ahead: he'd have to ask permission from his parents to work out with Cheeko. After all, he was a stranger, just like Mr. Baruth. Maybe they'd want to meet him first.

Some of the other questions that he'd lost in his excitement started popping up in his brain now.

What did that *C* on Cheeko's hat stand for?

Where did he live?

Would he come to all the Redbirds' games the way Mr. Baruth had?

Sylvester was so lost in his thoughts, he almost missed his own driveway. But the minute he walked into the kitchen, he blurted out everything in a rush of words.

"Whoa! Hold it!" his father said, holding up his

right hand like a traffic cop. "You met whom? Cheeko? Cheeko who?"

His mother walked into the kitchen and poured herself a glass of ice water from the dispenser on the refrigerator door.

She frowned. "Don't tell me you've met another mysterious stranger." She looked at Mr. Coddmyer and added, "Speaking of mysteries, you're home early. How come?"

"I worked through lunch and thought I'd put some time in the garden while there's light. They'll beep me if anything comes up," he replied. Mr. Coddmyer had a new job as a troubleshooter for a computer software company. He hardly ever went into his office, but got his assignments from calls that came through on his beeper.

Sylvester wasn't really listening to their talk. He was too eager to get permission to practice with Cheeko.

"Cheeko didn't tell me his last name," he said. "He just introduced himself and told me he'd be willing to help me improve my game, you know, hitting and everything."

His father looked skeptical. "Didn't I hear that song before? Only a year ago . . . about a Mr. Baruth?"

"Yes, Dad," Sylvester said. "Cheeko's a friend of Mr. Baruth's. I mean, that's what he told me."

"We never got to meet your Mr. Baruth," said Mrs. Coddmyer. "But I will say that he did help you become a better player. That home run streak was incredible. And now there's another angel out of the blue who wants to help you again?"

"Angel?" Sylvester echoed. "I don't know if I'd go *that* far . . ."

"Well, whatever he is," replied his mother. "Listen, instead of just sitting around, let's get started on dinner. One of you get out the lettuce, wash it, and give it a whirl in the spinner. Someone else please set the table."

"First she manages the clerks in her store, now she puts us to work." Mr. Coddmyer laughed. "Don't push too hard. We're liable to go on strike."

As they set about their chores, Mr. and Mrs. Coddmyer continued to talk about Cheeko.

"Maybe this Cheeko and Mr. Baruth are on some

kind of coaching circuit," Mr. Coddmyer suggested. "I never heard of it before, but nothing would surprise me."

"Then I can go out after supper and practice with him?" Sylvester pleaded.

"I suppose I could give up clipping the hedge to meet this new supercoach," Mr. Coddmyer said. "Right after supper, I'll go over to the field with you."

"I'd like to meet him, too," said Mrs. Coddmyer, sitting down at the table in front of the salad bowl. "But I have a huge inventory to go over tonight. It's going to take hours."

"That's okay, Mom," said Sylvester. "You can meet him if he comes to some Redbird games. Maybe you and Dad will be able to make a few more now." He'd never told them how much he missed seeing them in the stands this year. Maybe because he was a little embarrassed that he didn't get to play that much.

"By the way, why does Cheeko think you need help?" asked Mr. Coddmyer, dropping a pile of salad greens on his plate. "Has he seen you play?"

"I suppose so," said Sylvester. "I've never noticed him at a game, though."

"Gets more and more mysterious, our friend with the *C* on his cap," Mr. Coddmyer said with a frown. "I think . . ."

His thought was interrupted by the sound of his beeper. He shook his head as he went to dial the phone. Sylvester and his mother couldn't help overhearing him; the tone alone told them he wouldn't be finishing his meal, never mind going to watch his son practice.

"It's our biggest customer," he announced, hanging up the phone. "There's a major glitch in the system. I have to get over there right away."

"Can I still go practice with Cheeko, please?" Sylvester pleaded with both parents.

They glanced at each other in consultation.

"Well, all right," said his mother. "But only till it starts to get dark. Then you get right home, you hear?"

By the time she had finished saying that, Sylvester had picked up his glove and bat and was halfway out the door.

4

Sylvester was so eager to get to the field, he started to run the minute he reached the street. But after running nearly a block at a fast clip, he realized he might get tired and not perform as well as he should. So he slowed down to a brisk walk.

When he got to the field, Cheeko was already there, juggling three baseballs like someone in a carnival. There were three more balls on the ground next to him.

"Hi, Mr. Cheeko!" Sylvester greeted him.

Cheeko stopped juggling the balls and looked over at him. "Hi, yourself, kid," he said. "Hey, no mister stuff. It's just Cheeko."

"Okay," Sylvester smiled. "But . . ."

"No buts," said Cheeko. "You all set to hustle?"

"All set." Sylvester nodded.

"Good. First we'll work on your fielding. Take a hike out to center."

Sylvester dropped his bat and ran deep into the outfield, his heart light as a feather. Boy, am I lucky, he thought, to be chosen by an expert — Cheeko sure sounded like an expert — to get help in fielding and batting. He wished his folks could be here to see how professional Cheeko acted, too.

There was another thing running through his mind, too, maybe just as important: if he got better at bat, he might be able to give the wise guys on the team a little competition. Especially that smart-mouth, Trent Sturgis, who looked down on everyone as if he were king of the Redbirds. Nothing would make Sylvester happier, he thought, than to start outhitting that swellheaded punk.

"Here we go!" Cheeko shouted, and knocked an easy fly ball out to him. Nevertheless, Syl got under it at the wrong time and the ball hit the heel of his glove and dropped to the green turf.

In a split second, his feeling of joy changed to disappointment and embarrassment. He knew it should have been an easy catch, yet he'd flubbed it like a rookie.

"Never mind that one, Syl!" Cheeko called out to him. "Spilled milk. Get the next one. Keep your eye on the ball."

Cheeko hit the next one slightly lower than the first, forcing Sylvester to run in about eight or nine steps. This time he got both his bare hand and his glove on the ball, even though it struck just below the pocket. He was determined to hang on to it — and he did.

Little by little, Cheeko started hitting them higher, and to the left or the right, making each catch more difficult. In the beginning of this shift, Sylvester missed a few. But Cheeko kept up his stream of encouraging comments — "Don't worry about the other guys. If it's anywhere near you, go for it. Let 'em eat your dust. Hustle! Show 'em you're in charge out there. Step on 'em before they step on you."

He began to get the hang of it, and, after each catch, he gave himself a little mental pat on the back.

I'm getting better already, he told himself after about forty-five minutes of practice. I know I am.

"Okay, Syl," Cheeko called out to him a few minutes later. "That's enough of that for now."

His face glistening with sweat, Sylvester trotted in, smiling proudly. "How'd I do?" he asked.

Of course, he had his own opinion, but he wanted to know what Cheeko thought of his efforts.

"Good," said Cheeko. "Not perfect, but good. After all," he added, "you don't expect to be perfect right off, do you?"

"Sure can try." Sylvester laughed.

Cheeko laughed, too. "Right," he said seriously. "Grab your bat and get over there in front of the backstop screen." Then, turning to face the stands, he yelled, "Ladies and gentlemen, on the mound for the home team — the one and only —" he paused and he seemed to drift far away for an instant — "Cheeko! Batting leadoff for the opposition — Sylvester Coddmyer the third!"

Chuckling, he trotted out to the pitcher's mound. Cheeko didn't have a glove, but he wouldn't need one just to pitch.

As he trotted toward the batter's box, Syl felt Cheeko eyeing him. The would-be slugger tried to relax. Cheeko stretched, and delivered. Sylvester noticed that Cheeko was left-handed. The ball breezed in chest high. Sylvester swung at it as hard as he could. He missed it by a mile.

"Hey, hey, slow it down!" Cheeko called. He came off the mound toward Sylvester. "Don't be so anxious. Let's take one step back for a moment. First off, don't advertise to the pitcher that you're nervous. Give him the eye as you approach the batter's box; make him think you got him all figured out so nothing he throws at you will come as a surprise. Like this."

Cheeko took a few steps back, shouldered the bat, and stared at the pitcher's mound. His eyes never left that spot as he swaggered toward home plate and tapped the dirt from his sneakers. Boy, thought Syl, shivering, I sure wouldn't want to be on the receiving end of that stare.

Cheeko turned and handed him the bat with his usual wide smile. "Now you try it, Syl. Wait for me to get on the mound." He ran back to position and yelled, "Look real mean, but don't lose control. Keep your eye on the ball, but don't attack it. Okay, let's see your stuff!"

Syl shouldered the bat as Cheeko had done and

fixed his gaze on the left-handed pitcher. He pictured Trent and Bobby watching him and narrowed his eyes just a bit more. Cheeko tossed in another pitch, this one almost in the same spot as the first. Sylvester remembered his advice as he swung at it.

Crack! Bat met ball and sent it soaring to center field. It was one of the longest drives he'd hit since those over-the-fence homers he'd racked up last year. The throbbing in his chest returned.

Sturgis, get ready to eat dust! he wanted to shout.

"There you go," said Cheeko, nodding. "Caught on already. I knew you had it in you."

Sylvester smiled. Maybe that was my problem, he thought. I've been too anxious, wanting to kill the ball instead of just meeting it — and any pitcher could see that with no trouble at all.

He missed some of Cheeko's pitches but managed to connect with most of them. Some were grounders, some were fly balls to the outfield, and some even soared over the fence.

"Whew! All right, Sylvester," said Cheeko after two straight pitches ended up over the left field fence. "We'd better quit before we run out of baseballs. Not only that, but I'm getting winded."

"Can we get together again, Cheeko?" Sylvester asked hopefully.

"Of course. You don't expect to have it all after just one session, do you?"

"No, I don't."

"How about tomorrow, then? Same time, same place?"

"Sure if . . . if you don't mind."

"Mind?" said Cheeko, wiping his face with a bright red handkerchief. "Why should I mind?"

"Well," Sylvester hesitated owning up to what was troubling him. "I mean, I don't want to take up a lot of your time. I mean, there's lots of kids who could use help, so . . ."

"Sew buttons." Cheeko laughed. "Ever hear that one? Hey, listen, I pick who I want to help and that's that. As long as you listen to what I say, we'll get somewhere. There's more than one way to win a ball game."

"What do you mean?" asked Sylvester.

"You'll find out," said Cheeko. "There's still plenty to learn. Little shortcuts you won't find in books, believe me. So just show up tomorrow and we'll go at it again. Okay, pal?" He gave Sylvester a gentle poke in the ribs.

Sylvester grinned and threw out his hand for a high five. "Okay!"

Cheeko tilted his cap and headed off down the road in the opposite direction.

Sylvester wondered where he lived. There were no cars in the parking lot. Maybe he was staying at some motel within walking distance.

It was just starting to get dark as Sylvester picked up his bat and glove and started on his way. He couldn't help thinking about the future, when his practice sessions would, he hoped, pay off during some real games. Wouldn't it be dynamite if he could start getting home runs like last year? Super-dynamite! That would be better than getting a 100 on every test — history, spelling, and arithmetic included!

He was just about to cross an intersection a block from his house when a voice called out, "Sylvester! Wait a minute!"

Sylvester stopped, turned, and saw the familiar figure of Snooky Malone running toward him.

"Hey, where've you been?" Snooky asked.

Snooky had gone all the way through school with Sylvester since kindergarten. Sometimes they were real close friends. But lately Snooky had been more of a pain than a pal. With his great big wire-rimmed eyeglasses and his scruffy hair sticking out all over his head, Snooky looked like an owl. He tried to act wise, too, as if he knew it all, but he asked a million questions. Sylvester knew if he told him anything about what he'd just been doing, there'd be no letup. Snooky would pester him until Sylvester would be ready to strangle him.

"I was at the field. Hoped someone would show up to play a little, but nobody did," Sylvester admitted. He hoped this little white lie would hold Snooky off for a while.

Snooky glanced at his digital watch. "This time of day? I never saw anybody out at the field this time of day."

"Well, I just took a shot. You never know," said Sylvester, walking a little faster.

Snooky tagged along at his side.

"Hey, Sylvester, I was looking at your horoscope, you know, to see what the stars say, and . . ."

Sylvester stopped in his tracks. He didn't believe in star charts and stuff like that the way Snooky did, but he was a little curious at the moment. He played along with Snooky.

"Let me guess," he said. "They say my future looks good. That I'm heading for the top, just like last year. Right?"

Might as well take a shot, show him I know what he's all about, he thought, remembering Cheeko's advice. Couldn't do better than showing a little muscle to the wizard of the stars himself, one Snooky Malone.

"Well . . . yes . . . and no," Snooky replied, as though he weren't sure how to answer.

"Yes and no? What's that supposed to mean?"

"You're going to look good in some ways, but . . ." He paused, scratched his elbow, and stood there.

"But what?" asked Sylvester, suddenly impatient. Snooky usually wasn't at a loss for words.

"You won't like this, Syl, but I have to tell you. You're heading for some good things, but you're also asking for some trouble ahead."

"Trouble?" Sylvester frowned. "What kind of trouble?"

Snooky shrugged. "I don't know."

Sylvester snorted. "You're something else, you know that, Snooky? You're always into something, like reading bones, or fortune-telling cards, or tea leaves, or even stars. But you never have the full picture, that's your trouble. I'll tell you what's true — the first part. I am heading for some good things. And that's it. So sleep under the stars, Snooky. Maybe one of them will drop down and clue you in on what's happening now — never mind the future!"

Hiking his bat on his shoulder, he swaggered on down the street, leaving his old pal in a trail of dust.

5

At the Redbirds' practice the next afternoon, Sylvester could sense a big improvement in both his fielding and hitting — even though it didn't seem as if anyone else noticed. But he wasn't about to make a lot of noise about it. "Hey, guys, see me catch the ball? Anyone see that thump of the old beanbag?" That would grab attention, all right, but the worst kind.

All he had to do was keep it up and they'd see it. Eventually.

He could hardly wait to practice with Cheeko again.

That night, Mrs. Coddmyer was still struggling with her inventory figures. Mr. Coddmyer was working late. It seemed as though they'd never get to see Sylvester at bat again. Not even at practice.

He thought of asking Joyce to come watch but decided against it for now. It would be more fun to see the surprised look on her face after he started connecting with the ball in some actual games.

Cheeko was waiting for him on the field and they got right down to work. After a while, Sylvester could easily tell that he'd improved some more. Cheeko hit a lot of high fly balls and he caught most of them with ease. He hit a lot more of Cheeko's pitches, too. And there was no doubt about his accuracy. He was hitting long drives to the outfield, most of which cleared the fence by five to twenty feet.

"Hey, hey, pal, you're doin' pretty good," said Cheeko as they wound up for the evening. "I'd say you're about fifty percent better than yesterday. You're starting to get tougher, too. Meaner. Really digging in, you know. How're you feeling at the plate?"

"Great," said Sylvester, a little surprised at the question. He'd knocked so many over the fence, why shouldn't he feel great?

"I mean relaxing-wise," explained Cheeko, making fists of his hands and rolling his muscular shoulders back and forth. "Yesterday, you know, you were strung up tight as guitar strings. You a little looser today?"

"Oh, sure," replied Sylvester, understanding now what Cheeko meant. No big deal, he thought.

"Good, good," said Cheeko, tapping him on the shoulders. "You never want to let the suckers know you're nervous or anything, pal. Now look, I want to show you just a couple more things. Get out there and throw a few pitches."

"I'll never be a pitcher, Cheeko," Sylvester protested.

"No sweat, I just want you to look at what I do when the ball gets a little close," said Cheeko.

And as Sylvester threw one ball after another toward the plate, Cheeko taught him how to lean in just enough to let the ball graze him — and then fall down as though he were in agony. He did it in such a way the ump would never be able to tell it was faked.

Sylvester wasn't sure he'd ever be able to do that — it looked a bit dangerous — but it was another lesson. Besides, a little physical pain might be worth it, if it got Trent and the others off his case.

When it was over, Cheeko wiped off his forehead.

"So, I'll see you again tomorrow night, right?"

Sylvester smiled. "Right."

Suddenly a light bulb popped on in his head. "Oh, I can't!" he said. "Tomorrow's Friday, and we're playing the Lansing Wildcats!"

"No problem." Cheeko shrugged. "We can get together Saturday morning, say around nine. Okay?"

"Sure. Will you be at the game tomorrow?"

"Wild horses couldn't keep me away," Cheeko replied with a big smile.

"Great. Well, see you then. Or, you'll see me!"

"You betcha," Cheeko said, and they parted company.

Sylvester didn't want to bump into Snooky Malone again, even accidentally, so he took a different route home. Snooky seemed to have a knack for showing up at the oddest places at just the wrong time. In fact, it was surprising that he hadn't been at the field this evening. Probably home gazing into a crystal ball . . . or watching *Star Trek* reruns. Yeah, he really freaked out on anything to do with the stars.

The next morning, Sylvester woke to discover a lazy drizzle falling. By noon he began to worry that it might be bad enough to postpone the game. With his gut feeling that he'd improved to the point where he could make a difference out there, the last thing he wanted to happen was a postponement.

But by mid-afternoon the sky had cleared, the sun had come out, and the stands filled up quickly with impatient Wildcat and Redbird fans. Sylvester could almost hear his heart singing "Take Me Out to the Ball Game," even though his stomach was so fidgety he couldn't even think about peanuts or Cracker Jack!

Chances were he'd probably sit out the first three or four innings on the bench. After all, he hadn't started since that one day back when Coach Corbin had to use him because only eight players had shown up.

With these thoughts running through his head, he got through infield and batting practice quietly and quickly. Then the field was cleared and the game was ready to begin.

Glove on his lap, arms crisscrossed over his chest, Sylvester sat in the middle of the dugout so that he had a good view of both the first base and third base sides of the bleachers. With the small crowd out there, it wouldn't be too difficult to spot Cheeko, he thought, unless his new pal had decided to sit somewhere directly behind him. No Cheeko came into view. That must be it.

The Lansing Wildcats, in their fresh, clean, white-trimmed green uniforms, were up at bat first.

As the Hooper Redbirds, in their bright red white-trimmed uniforms, took the field to a roar of cheers from their fans, a shadow appeared in front of Sylvester.

"Syl! Look sharp! Sorry, I forgot to tell you, kid, but I want you to start in right field today."

Was he dreaming already? No, it was Coach Corbin, peering down at him.

Sylvester blinked as though he'd come out of a fog, then sprang out of the dugout as if he'd been shot from a gun. He ran about ten yards before he realized what a break this was. Turning around, he shouted back, "Thanks, Coach!"

Coach Corbin smiled. "Just do what you've been doing in practice," he said calmly.

Sylvester ignored the sudden rush of butterflies to his stomach and took his position at right field — where Les Kendall usually played. He pounded his fist into the pocket of his glove and shouted to the pitcher, Rick Wilson. "Get 'im outta there, Rick, ol' buddy! Make it one, two, three, guy!"

Mickey Evans, leading off for the Wildcats, watched two of right-hander Wilson's pitches blaze by him for a ball and a strike before he cocked the third pitch to short right field.

It was high and hard to see where it would come down. Sylvester sprinted after it, groaning in dismay that the very first hit had come his way.

He reached the ball in time to extend his glove — and caught it to make the first out.

There was a resounding cheer from the Redbirds' fans. It made him feel that he was back in the mainstream after wading in the shallows for so long. The cheers really raised his spirits.

Short, stalwart Georgie Talman stepped to the plate next. He took two balls and two strikes, then struck out. Two away.

Bongo Daley, the Wildcats' burly right-handed pitcher, was also their cleanup hitter. He lived up to his nickname as he slammed a two-bagger to right center field between Bobby Kent and Sylvester. Bobby got to the ball first and pegged it to second

45

base to keep Bongo from stretching his hit to a triple. He never even glanced at Sylvester as they both got ready for the next batter.

Sylvester tried to ignore him, too. As tall, skinny Ken Tilton came to bat, he yelled, "C'mon, Rick! Get 'im outta there!"

Bobby, Ted Sobel in left field, and the entire infield joined in shouting encouragement.

Their yells didn't help. Ken singled, scoring Bongo. Then Leon Hollister, the Wildcats' third baseman, connected with a triple, scoring Ken. Finally, Rod Piper grounded out to end the two-run half inning.

"Okay, guys, are we gonna let those Wildcats get away with two runs? Or are we gonna do somethin' about it?" Coach Corbin shouted to his players.

"We're gonna do somethin' about it!" The answer came out loud and clear, as if from one powerful throat.

But the first two batters, Jim Cowley and Ted Sobel, hit pop flies for easy outs. Then Trent singled over first, and Sylvester, batting cleanup, approached the plate. His hands felt clammy, but he held the bat with confidence.

He stared down the pitcher and took the first pitch.

Crack! A high, long, cloud-piercing shot to deep left field! And over the fence for a home run!

The fans rose in their seats, cheered, whistled, and clapped wildly as Sylvester Coddmyer III trotted around the bases for the first time that season. He hadn't felt so good since last year, and that seemed so long, long ago.

Just about the whole team met him at home plate. They exchanged high fives and slapped him on the back, shouting "Way to go!" and stuff like that. He noticed a few who didn't come near him. Trent didn't make a move. And Bobby wasn't exactly jumping up and down, either.

Get used to it, guys, Sylvester thought. There's more where that one came from.

He turned and looked into the stands above the dugout. The space where his parents usually sat was empty, but at the end of the first row of the bleachers toward the first base side, he saw who he was looking for.

Proudly, he waved to Cheeko, who whistled and waved back.

The Wildcats got another run in the top of the second, and another in the third, putting them in the lead 4–2.

Then, in the bottom of the third, with two out and nobody on, Sylvester came up to bat again.

He tapped the plate and thought, No sweat, as he listened to the cheering fans. A question flashed through his mind — Was one of those voices Joyce's?

"Knock it out of the park, Sylvester!"

"Drive it into the next county, Syl!"

He didn't. He never even touched the ball with his bat. After two called strikes that whistled by him, he swung at a third right down the middle and struck out.

6

Head bowed, eyes glued to the turf, Sylvester headed back to the dugout. He was so embarrassed he wished he could say a magic word and vanish.

He'd had three good, over-the-plate pitches. How could he have missed them all?

The Wildcats' fans laughed and mocked him with phony applause. The Redbirds' fans remained mute, as if they were stunned. How could their cleanup batter, who had hit a home run his first time up, swing at three pitches and miss every time?

None of the guys said a word to him as they picked up their gloves and headed out to the field. He avoided Trent's eyes. He could just imagine the smile he'd see in them, and the smirk on Bobby's face.

He grabbed his glove and trotted out to right

field, passing the Redbirds' first baseman, Jerry Ash, on the way. Jerry called, "Figure you were just lucky that first time, huh, Syl?"

Thanks a lot, thought Sylvester. What about my home run? I guess Jerry forgot that he struck out his first time up. Maybe that's what I ought to do now, just forget it.

But he couldn't. Sullen and ashamed, he sneaked a look into the stands at where he'd seen Cheeko. He wondered if his new pal had become disappointed, too, and left.

But Cheeko was still there, watching the Wildcats' first batter, who was approaching the plate.

The batter, A. C. Compton, fanned after six pitches. Mickey Evans went down swinging, too, drawing applause from the Redbirds' fans.

Then Georgie Talman, after fouling off four straight pitches, was given four straight balls, and walked.

Bongo Daley's fans gave him a rousing cheer as he stepped into the batter's box. It was plain that the tall, hefty blond pitcher was a favorite with the Wildcats' fans.

Bongo missed Rick's first pitch, but sliced the next

one out between right and center fields. The slice took it on a curve directly toward Sylvester, who raced after it with lead weights pounding in his chest. It looked as though it might hit the ground before he got there, but he dove at it the very last second — and caught it as the back of his gloved hand touched the turf. Three out.

The Redbirds' fans cheered him as he ran off the field, tossing that ball into his glove again and again. He shot a brief glance toward Cheeko and saw him applauding along with the crowd.

Sylvester felt great. So what if that catch didn't make up for his strikeout? Hey, it kept another run from scoring, didn't it?

He'd barely settled down in the dugout, this time at the far end, when he heard a voice at his side say, "Hi, Sylvester!"

It was Snooky Malone.

"What are you doing here, Snooky?" he asked. "You're not on the team."

"Coach Corbin doesn't mind," said Snooky. "I did his horoscope for him. He's a Libra, nice and even tempered."

"Good for him," muttered Sylvester. I wonder

what the sign is for a pest. That must be Snooky's sign, he thought.

"I just can't get over it, Syl," Snooky whispered.

"Over what?" Sylvester asked, softly, as though Snooky was in on a big secret.

"The way you're hitting. And the way you're not. And that catch. You haven't made a catch like that since last year, when you won that trophy, remember?"

"Look, Snooky." Syl's voice rose slightly. "I don't know what's with you these days, but lay off, huh? Don't bug me anymore."

Snooky frowned at him. "I know your sign, Sylvester. You're a Gemini. Geminis are great at whatever they do, and you prove it. Except for one thing."

"Oh, yeah? What?"

"What happened between last year and this year? You were hot and then you were cold and now you're getting hot again. I can't figure it," Snooky replied, his eyebrows raised high above his big wire-rimmed glasses.

"I don't know," Sylvester snapped. "And I don't care."

He nudged Snooky with his elbow and almost knocked him over.

"Scram, will you, Snook?" he said. "You're getting into my hair and I want to concentrate on the game."

"And another thing," Snooky said, ignoring him. "Who'd you wave at in the stands? Was it . . ."

"None of your business!" Sylvester growled. "Beat it, will you? Or do I have to throw you out?"

Heads and eyes swung around and stared down at his end of the bench. He felt his face turn bright red. Darn that Snooky for barging in and reminding him how terrible he'd played this year. Why couldn't he keep his nose out of other people's business?

"I'll tell you one thing, Sylvester Coddmyer the Third," said Snooky, getting up to go. "You're heading for deep trouble."

And then he was gone.

Sylvester settled back, trying to forget the pesky runt. Deep trouble? What did that mean? Maybe a star had fallen on Snooky's pointed little head!

He turned his attention to the leadoff batter, Jerry Ash, who took a swing at a high pitch.

"Strike!" called the ump.

Five pitches later, Jerry walked, bringing up

Bobby Kent. For the good of the team, Sylvester thought, I hope you get on base, Bobby.

Bobby waited out the pitches, then rapped a ground skimmer down to second. Mickey fielded it, touched second base, then pegged it to first for a quick double play.

"Oh, no!" the Redbirds' fans groaned.

Sylvester was secretly ashamed that he didn't feel as bad as he probably should have for Bobby. But he was still half thinking about Snooky as he watched his pal Duane Francis fly out to deep center to end the inning.

A Gemini, Snooky had called him. So what? What had being a Gemini done for him lately? Nothing. It's what you do for yourself, he remembered Cheeko telling him. He had to take care of Number One.

That put a little pep into him as he picked up his glove and headed out to his field position. After all, he was still in the game. Coach Corbin hadn't lost faith in him. Why shouldn't he still make a few waves in this game?

7

Ken Tilton, the Wildcats' powerhouse, was up. So far he'd rapped out a single and a double. With his eagle eye and strength, he could easily pull in a triple this time at bat.

Coach Corbin motioned the outfielders to move back, and they did. Obviously, the coach wasn't taking any chances on Ken's hitting.

Rick toed the rubber, then sent a blazing pitch just inside the plate, brushing Ken off. Ken jumped back to avoid being hit as the ump called "Ball!"

The next pitch was outside. The next was inside again, but not as close to Ken as the first. Three balls and no strikes.

Was a walk better than giving Ken something to swing at? Glad I'm not the pitcher, Sylvester thought.

Then, "Strike!" A streaking fastball over the inside corner.

Another "Strike!" as Rick fired again.

Ken stepped out of the box, rubbed the heavy part of his bat a couple of times, and stepped back in.

The windup. The pitch. Crack! Ken connected and sent the ball soaring out to right field.

Sylvester could see it shoot high into the sky like a tiny rocket and then start to arc down. He could tell right off that it was going over his head, so he wasted no time. He turned and ran back toward the fence as fast as his legs could carry him.

The old fear gripped him. Could he get to it in time? The fence would be in his way. He'd miss it by a mile.

But at the very last moment, just as the ball came down over his head, he leapt, his gloved hand stretched out as far as it could possibly go.

Thud! He hit the fence way up high — and caught the ball.

Pain pierced his shoulders like a bolt of lightning, but it didn't last long. Joy sprang into his heart as soon as he was back on his feet. As he heaved the ball into the infield, he could hear the crowd's roar that had started the instant he'd snagged the ball; it didn't die down for a good minute. In fact, everyone was standing up and cheering, Redbirds' and Wildcats' fans alike. They didn't get to see too many catches like that.

As Sylvester stood out in right field, arms crossed over his chest, he remembered Cheeko's advice: play tough, go for it. He was determined not to forget that.

He scanned the crowd, hoping to spot his mom and dad in their usual place. They had both said they'd try to make the game this time, but it was hard to predict with their busy work schedules. He couldn't pick them out, but he caught a glimpse of Joyce, all smiles and happy. And there was Cheeko in his usual spot.

Before he could pick anyone else out in the crowd, Leon Hollister came up to bat. He'd tripled in the first inning and flied out in the third. This time he waited for a full count, then laced a high fly ball to short center field. Bobby had plenty of time and got under it for the second out.

When the ball left Leon's bat, Sylvester had

started toward it and then was relieved when he saw that it was an easy stand-up catch for Bobby. He was beginning to have doubts about fly balls. They might not all end up in his glove like the last one. His confidence began to ebb slowly.

Rod Piper was up next. After two strikes, both of them foul balls that rolled down the backstop screen, he took four straight balls and walked.

Next up was Russ Skelton, the Wildcats' tall, wiry shortstop. So far Russ had been on base each time up. Sylvester remembered that he'd walked his first time and singled the second time. Not bad for the seventh batter in the lineup, Sylvester thought.

He shook out his arms and shoulders and got ready for whatever Russ might hit his way. After two pitches, the third one was hit to Trent, who scooped it up and pegged it to first. Sylvester could relax as he ran off the field.

As he passed by Cheeko, he saw his friend wave at him and give the air in front of him a short poke with his fist. Sylvester smiled, knowing that this meant to get tough. He waved back at Cheeko.

If his folks had been there, he could have introduced them to Cheeko so they would be comfortable about all those practice sessions. Once they met him and talked with him, they might even want to come to Sylvester's games and sit with him.

But first things first. The first batter hadn't left the dugout before Sylvester started worrying about what would happen if he came to bat this inning. Would he get a decent hit? Or would he disgrace himself? Even with Cheeko's coaching, he still wasn't as confident as last year when Mr. Baruth had been around.

Maybe he was too impatient. Maybe he expected too much too soon. Maybe maybe maybe.

He wiped these thoughts out of his mind as he settled down on a vacant seat in the dugout.

"C'mon, guys!" Coach Corbin said, walking back and forth and clapping his hands loudly. "We can't give up now! Hey, we're only two runs down! And they're not that good. So go out there and prove it to 'em, okay?"

"Okay!" the whole team shouted.

"Good! Okay, Eddie! Start it rollin'!"

He headed toward the third base coaching box.

Eddie Exton removed his catcher's gear, put on a helmet, carefully selected a bat, and strode to the plate.

As Eddie readied himself for the first pitch, Duane Francis nudged Sylvester. "Hey, Syl, I forgot to tell you, my dad took me to a big baseball card show last Sunday."

Sylvester had a small collection of baseball cards that he'd picked up here and there. Duane was definitely in the big league as a collector and went out of his way to fill in gaps, especially with old, old cards and players you hardly ever heard about. He loved to share his finds, and Sylvester enjoyed seeing them.

"I got a whole bunch of really great old ones," Duane went on, "Red Sox, White Sox, Black Sox . . ."

"Black Sox?" Sylvester was puzzled.

"Yeah, it's a nickname they gave a bunch of Chicago guys," said Duane. "Hey, wanna take a look at them later?"

"Sure," said Sylvester. "Bring them over to my house after supper."

Sylvester turned his attention to home plate just in time to see Eddie pop out to third base. One out.

The Redbirds' fans were getting restless. "Let's get some hits!" they shouted.

Sure, thought Sylvester, easier said than done.

As Rick headed toward the plate, the Redbirds' pitcher seemed to have lost some of his energy. His shoulders were slumped and he gazed at the grounds as if his eyes were about to close down.

Don't fall asleep, Rick, Sylvester felt like yelling. We need you more than ever right now.

As the innings piled up, the Wildcats' two-run lead seemed harder and harder to match, never mind pass. And as one batter followed another, a little voice inside Sylvester's head kept asking the same agonizing question: "Is the coach going to take me out?"

As long as he was in there playing, there was hope that he might come through for the team.

Rick grounded out to shortstop.

Then Jim Cowley came up, and Sylvester crossed his fingers. He usually thought superstitions were silly — black cats and broken mirrors and all that star stuff of Snooky's — but things looked so bad, he figured it was worth a try.

Jim let a strike go by, fouled the next pitch, then fanned. It was a fast, unproductive fifth inning.

"Rats!" Sylvester snorted as he uncrossed his fingers and started out of the dugout. "I knew it was baloney!"

One more inning to go. The way Bongo Daley was pitching for the Wildcats, it looked as though it would be no different from the last scoreless four.

"Come on, you guys!" Coach Corbin pleaded as his team headed for their field positions. "If you can't hit 'em, at least hold 'em!"

The coach was not in a happy mood. He hated to lose.

We're doing our best, Coach, Sylvester thought as he trotted out to right field. At least I am.

8

Les Easton, the Wildcats' short and stocky right fielder, was first man up. He watched six pitches streak by him, two strikes and four balls, to put him on base.

Next up was A. C. Compton. He walked, too.

Great, thought Sylvester, they're already winning and Rick is making it easy for them to pick up at least two more runs.

Before stepping into the batter's box, Mickey Evans swung the bat around his head a few times like an Olympic javelin ace preparing for a record throw. So far he'd managed one hit, a single, but he was always dangerous enough to pull a repeat.

He didn't. With one strike on him, he slammed the next pitch a mile high, almost directly over home plate, and Eddie Exton made the catch look easy.

Sylvester breathed a small sigh of relief. One out. Two to go.

Georgie Talman, the next batter, tried to play it smart, waiting out the pitches to the very last. But Rick remained ahead with one ball and two strikes on Georgie before he breezed one in almost a little too low to be in the strike zone. But Georgie, not wanting to risk being called out, swung. He smashed a grass-mowing grounder down to short. Trent fielded it neatly, whipped it to third, and got Les out by ten feet.

Two out. One more to go. But this one wasn't going to be easy. Bongo Daley had doubled in the first inning, and it was just bad luck that his other two outs — both fly balls — hadn't landed between the outfielders. He was powerful enough to blast one easily over the fence.

Sylvester joined his teammates in a chant of encouragement to their pitcher, at the same time backing up a few steps. Rick glanced at the runner on second base, then threw.

Bong stepped into it, but let it go by.

"Strike!" boomed the ump.

"Way to go, Rick!" Sylvester yelled. "Mow 'im down, kid! Show 'im who's in charge!"

Act tough, sound tough, wasn't that what Cheeko had been teaching him?

The next pitch missed the plate by inches. Then Rick committed a serious error — he threw one in the dirt that skipped by Eddie and headed for the backstop screen.

"Oh, no!" Sylvester moaned, as Eddie sprang to his feet, whirled, and bolted after the wild ball. He caught it as it bounced back from the screen, then whipped it to Rick, who had come in to cover home plate.

But the runner on second had stopped on third. He'd only been off the base a short, safe distance when Rick swung around toward him. The runner on first, meanwhile, had advanced to second.

Boy, that's just great, Sylvester grumbled to himself. He could picture another run or two scoring easily, as he saw Coach Corbin walk out to the mound. After a few seconds, he patted Rick on the shoulder, then trotted slowly off the field.

Sylvester wondered whether the coach should

have taken Rick out, but he gave no indication. Never show the suckers you're scared, that was another bit of Cheeko's advice.

Still standing tall on the mound, Rick again checked the runners, then delivered. The pitch was in there, and Bongo swung. Crack! It was a long, high fly to right center field.

Almost before the sound of the bat meeting the ball faded, Sylvester started running toward it as fast as he possibly could, all the while hoping it would be Bobby's ball.

Then he heard Bobby's clear, unquestionable call: "Take it, Syl! It's all yours!"

Take it? Was Bobby crazy? He didn't have a chance. No way! It was Bobby's ball, not his!

But he had to try. He picked up more speed, though where it came from he was sure he didn't know. Besides, since Bobby had dumped it on him, he *had* to do his best, even collapse in the attempt.

At the very last moment, as the ball was dropping fast in front of him, he dove at it — and grabbed it in his gloved hand.

For one split second, his mitt turned over from the impact and it felt as though the ball had wobbled out. But Sylvester recovered his wits and slid his glove forward, and showed the ball still inside, as though it had always been there.

He lay on the turf for a moment, to catch his breath, as the cheers and whistles from the fans echoed and reechoed throughout the park.

Finally, he pushed himself to his feet, rubbed some of the grass off the front of his uniform, and jogged off the field.

As he ran, he glanced at Cheeko, who was standing and cheering with the fans. Sylvester could tell that Cheeko had seen *everything* and approved the way he had "recovered" the catch.

Some of the guys shook his hand as he reached the dugout. Coach Corbin was beaming. "Another fantastic catch, Syl!"

Even Bobby Kent came up to him this time and gave him a high five. "I knew it was your ball, Syl," he admitted. "No way I could've gotten to it. You really surprised me out there!"

"Surprised myself!" Sylvester laughed.

"Okay, last chance," cried the coach. "Let's show 'em we're not licked yet! Billy, call 'em off."

As Coach Corbin headed down to the third base

coaching box, Billy Haywood called off the names of the first three batters: "Sobel! Sturgis! Coddmyer!"

Sylvester's ears perked up at the sound of his name. He'd forgotten that he'd be batting this last half of the sixth inning — the last inning and the last chance to win the game. It seemed a pretty dim possibility, practically impossible, the way things had been going.

Ted, who had flied out his first two times up, fouled off the first two pitches, putting himself into a hole right off. A swing and a miss now would mean the first out.

As Sylvester clenched his fists and watched the action at the plate, a familiar voice beside him whispered loudly, "I can't believe what you're doing out there, Sylvester. It's like you're a different person, not the Sylvester Coddmyer the Third I've know all these years!"

For a second, he panicked. Had someone seen him bobble the ball during that final catch?

The voice, now recognizable as Snooky's, went on, though, with no reference to that questionable moment.

"You were great last year, of course. And you're

playing great now. But what happened in between? I mean you were just plain lousy a week ago."

Snooky had managed to squeeze in on the bench beside Sylvester again. And there he was, asking those same, tired questions.

"I don't know, okay?" replied Sylvester. "Look, maybe I'm just on another streak. What's your problem with that? Can't a guy get lucky more than once?"

"Yeah, but . . . this is different, Sylvester. I can tell it isn't just luck." Snooky persisted, squinting over his thick glasses to examine his neighbor on the bench. "You've changed somehow. You have a different attitude. Yep, trouble. I can see trouble, Syl."

Sylvester leaned forward and stared Snooky hard in the eyes. "Snooky, will you just shut up? Mind your own business, will you? Get off my back and take your stupid stars with you. I'm fed up with you, get it? I'm fed right up to here," Sylvester said, placing his hand under his chin.

Snooky stared back, as if he were trying to read something in Sylvester's eyes. Then, without another word, he hitched up his sagging jeans and left the dugout to return to the stands.

That creep, Sylvester thought. Is he going to be on my case for the rest of my life?

He tried to thrust the little inquisitive pest out of his mind as much as possible. He leaned forward and concentrated on watching the game.

As Ted fouled off another pitch, he saw the umpire's fingers come up to reveal the count. Two balls, two strikes.

Then, a surprise — Bongo missed the plate with his next two pitches, and Ted walked.

Looking as if he hadn't a care in the world, Trent then stepped to the plate. He hadn't done that well in this game — a single and an easy grounder for an out — but he was always a threat to the opposition. And despite his nasty attitude toward him, Sylvester admired his batting ability.

"You're up next, Sylvester," Billy Haywood reminded him.

Sylvester started at the sound of his name. He blamed his forgetfulness on Snooky Malone's blathering. Somewhat flustered, he stepped out of the dugout, put on his helmet, picked out his favorite bat, and walked to the on-deck circle.

Trent waited until the count went to two balls and

two strikes before he cracked a sizzling grounder between third and short for a hit. The crowd cheered as Ted advanced to second base and Trent toed the bag at first. Sylvester stepped up to the plate and narrowed his eyes at Bongo.

"Okay, Sylvester! Hit it out of the park!"

The shout broke Sylvester's concentration. It came from that pesky, but still faithful, fan, none other than Snooky Malone, who was standing up on his seat and waving his hands in the air. Others chimed in, too, and Sylvester realized he was starting to get nervous as he stood in the batter's box.

"Strike!" called the ump as Bongo breezed in the first pitch.

"Str . . ." the umpire started to say as the next pitch rolled in down the middle. But Sylvester swung at it, made the connection, and sent the ball zooming out to deep left. It curved and just missed the foul line by about a foot.

"Foul ball!" yelled the ump.

"Make the next one count, Sylvester!" cried Snooky, jumping up and down on his seat.

Sylvester obliged. He lambasted the ball to almost the same spot where he'd hit the previous pitch —

except that this time it was an easy three feet to the right of the foul line pole.

Every Redbirds fan was up and cheering, giving Sylvester an ovation that could be heard in every corner of town. He spied his parents in their usual spot, applauding loudly with the others. His heart throbbed with such pride, he thought it would burst.

As he trotted around first base, he heard Russ Skelton, the shortstop, sneer. "Lucky break, Coddmyer. He threw ya' a meatball!"

Meatball, huh? Sylvester wasn't about to let him get away with that. On his way around the infield, he made a big loop and managed to give that loudmouth a nasty jab in the ribs in passing. Act tough, right? Isn't that what Cheeko would have done?

"Oof!" he heard Russ groan at the surprise poke. Sylvester just smiled and continued merrily on his way around third and then home.

Hooper Redbirds 5, Lansing Wildcats 4.

9

Sylvester could hardly believe the shouting, the cheers, the jostling, as the fans came streaming down onto the field.

"Syl! You were fabulous!" Joyce cried as she threw her arms around him. "But what happened with Russ out there?"

Oh, she noticed, he thought. So what? You have to be aggressive. That's what he'd learned from Cheeko.

Before he could explain all that, she got swept off in the crowd and was pointing him out to a bunch of her girlfriends.

Even some Wildcats fans were coming down to shake his hand. It was like a dream, a wonderful dream that had happened before, thanks to Mr. Baruth, and now was happening again thanks to someone else.

And there he was. Cheeko appeared out of the blue and stood next to him, grinning from ear to ear, holding out his hand for a high five.

"Nice, that last one, really nice," Cheeko said. "You're coming along great, kid."

"I owe it to you, Cheeko," said Sylvester, slapping his outstretched palm. "Every hit of it. I sure forgot everything I learned last year, but you brought it all back and then some. You showed me how to field, how to hit again, and . . ."

"Hey, you're the guy who does the work," Cheeko cut in. "And I like the way you got that shortstop." He chuckled softly. "You're learning. Look, I gotta run. Don't forget our practice session tomorrow morning. Same place as usual, okay?"

Sylvester quickly nodded as Cheeko started to leave.

He watched Cheeko thread his way through the crowd. Suddenly he remembered something and yelled after him. "Cheeko! Wait a sec!"

But his voice was drowned out by the noise all around him. Anyway, Cheeko was gone. Just like that he seemed to have vanished.

Sylvester felt the disappointment deep in the pit

of his stomach. He was anxious for his parents to meet Cheeko. It would mean a lot to him if they could get to know the one who had worked with him and shown him the *real* ins and outs of baseball.

Even as he was thinking about them, his mother and father got through the crowd and embraced him. They were so excited, he couldn't tell whether they were flushed or they'd been crying. It almost brought tears to his own eyes, but he bit his lip and hugged them back.

"Rats, I wanted you to meet him," Sylvester said, "but he's gone now."

"Meet who?" Mr. Coddmyer asked. "The coach? We've met him lots of times."

"No, Cheeko," said Sylvester. "He was here, but he had to leave."

"Another elusive mentor," said Mrs. Coddmyer. "Maybe some other time, when it's not so crowded."

"Yeah, okay," said Sylvester lamely.

"Sylvester?"

He turned. There stood Snooky, holding out his hand.

"I'm not angry even though you were kind of mean to me," said Snooky. "And I want to congratulate

75

you. You came through in a pinch. You did really great. No matter what's going on, I have to say that I admire you."

"Thanks, Snooky," Sylvester said, slapping the little guy's outstretched palm. "Hey, listen, I gotta go. See you around."

Snooky tugged at Sylvester's uniform shirt. "One more thing I noticed," he went on. "I saw you poke Skelton as you went by him. Isn't that kinda dirty playing?"

Sylvester thought for a quick moment, then looked him in the eyes and said, "No. Just smart."

He darted through the crowd, found his folks, and drove off with them in a pink cloud.

Back home, his father shook his head and said, "I've never seen you hit that way, Syl. I mean last year you were driving in home runs, but this year, that power is breathtaking. When did my son become such a slugger?" he joked.

Sylvester smiled back at him. "You might be in for some surprises, Dad. If you got to see more of my games . . ."

"Now that's a curve ball if ever I saw one," said Mr. Coddmyer, still in a good mood.

"No, really, you know what I mean. Anyhow, I think it's the help I've gotten from Cheeko. He pointed out a lot of things, like how I should stand at the plate, how to swing at the ball, how to be more aggressive. He said I was wimping out a little, that I had to take a really full swing."

"Well, I don't see you play that often," said Mrs. Coddmyer, "but I always thought you took a full swing."

"So did I," agreed Mr. Coddmyer. "But look, we're no experts like Cheeko. He must have been some player himself. What team did you say he played on?"

"I never asked him," said Sylvester. "But he had to have been in the pros. Let's see, *C*, that could be for Cleveland, or Cincinnati, or Chicago."

"Or Cooperstown," suggested Mr. Coddmyer. "Maybe he's in the Baseball Hall of Fame!"

"A lot of choices there," said Mrs. Coddmyer. "I'll tell you one thing. From what I heard all around me today, that catch of yours in the sixth inning should be in a Hall of Fame."

"Aw, Mom, you're prejudiced," said Sylvester.

"I have an idea," said Mrs. Coddmyer. "Why don't we go out for dinner? I'm not up to cooking."

"Neither am I," said Mr. Coddmyer.

"Neither am I," echoed Sylvester.

They all laughed and headed for the car.

When they returned home, Sylvester picked up his glove and cleaned off little bits of dirt and grass that had sneaked into the crevices. He then got out the special oil he used to keep the leather soft and supple in the right places. As he worked on it, his mind wandered to his two lucky breaks. Last year there was Mr. Baruth and this year Cheeko. Mr. Baruth was gone and he'd never gotten around to asking him a lot of questions. He wasn't going to let that happen with Cheeko. He was as curious as his parents to know more about him.

The phone interrupted his thoughts. "I'll get it," he shouted.

It was Duane Francis.

"Syl, you had some day!" Duane exclaimed. "Keep it up and you'll end up on a baseball card."

"Got a little way to go." Sylvester laughed. "So, are you coming over? I want to see what you got last Sunday."

"I'll be there in a jif," said Duane and hung up.

True to his word, Duane arrived at the Coddmyer house in less than ten minutes. In his hands he held a bulging shoebox, tied with an extralong shoelace.

"Come on in here," said Sylvester. He led Duane into the dining room with its big polished mahogany table. "We can spread them out on top. Just don't put anything wet or scratchy down. Mom will have a fit."

Mrs. Coddmyer called from the next room where she was curled up with a magazine on the couch, "I heard that. And you're absolutely right!"

Mr. Coddmyer put on a CD and tuned out in his favorite chair, only half aware of the chatter in the adjacent room.

Duane opened the box, removed a stack of cards that were held together by a rubber band, and picked up the top card.

"These are the Detroit Tigers," he explained, "and this one is Ty Cobb, one of the greatest. Look at his average."

"Wow! Three sixty-seven," Sylvester read aloud. "I didn't know he played with the Philadelphia A's, too."

"That's 'cause you're not really into the old-timers,

like I am," said Duane seriously. "That's where the really interesting stuff is."

"Maybe you're right," said Sylvester. "Let's take a look at some more."

Duane put Ty Cobb to one side and picked up another and read off the statistics. This was Rudy York, who hit eighteen home runs in the month of August 1937.

"Eighteen in one month!" Sylvester echoed. "Amazing!"

Duane grinned at him. "You almost did that last year, yourself. Remember? Probably would have if we played more than once a week."

Sylvester grinned broadly. How could he ever forget that season?

They went through the stack of Tigers cards and went on to the Red Sox and then the New York Yankees, one of Duane's biggest piles.

"Roger Maris!" Sylvester half-shouted as they came across that familiar face. "I know all about him. He busted Babe Ruth's home run record by one run!"

"Not officially."

"Well . . . right. He did play in more games in one season than the Babe."

"Hey, who said you don't know anything about old-timers!" Duane picked up another card. "Know who this is?"

Sylvester looked at the picture on the card and gasped.

"That looks like Mr. Baruth!" he choked.

"Hey, calm down," said Duane. "You all right?"

Sylvester nodded as he stared at the card, at the face of the big man in the striped uniform, wearing a hat with *NY* on it. Underneath the picture was the name "George Herman 'Babe' Ruth."

"He looks *exactly* like Mr. Baruth," Sylvester said, in a hoarse voice.

"Mr. Who?"

"Baruth," Sylvester repeated.

It did. It really did look like him.

Sylvester took the card and read the statistics on the back. He saw that George Herman "Babe" Ruth had retired from baseball in 1935 and died in 1948. That was years and years ago.

Then who . . . how . . . what . . . ?

"Who's this Mr. Baruth, anyhow?" asked Duane, curious.

"He's the guy who taught me how to hit and play

the outfield last year," Sylvester answered, still puzzling over the picture.

"You never mentioned him before," said Duane. "But, boy, that name . . ."

"I know," Sylvester interrupted. "Sounds a lot like 'Babe Ruth,' doesn't it?"

"Sure does."

"But it can't be. The Babe died in 1948."

"Must be some kind of gag or something," offered Duane. "Guy looks like Babe Ruth, so everyone calls him Baruth."

"Yeah, maybe that's it," murmured Sylvester. He really didn't know what to think.

They finished off the Yankees and moved on to another stack. This was the Chicago White Sox.

Duane started with the oldest ones and, before he got very far, he passed one over to Sylvester that almost knocked his friend off his chair.

"Wait a minute!" Sylvester shouted, waving the card in front of Duane's nose. "This one looks like Cheeko!"

"Cheeko? Who's Cheeko?"

"He's the guy who's helping me *this* year!"

10

The man on the card in the White Sox uniform wore a hat just like Cheeko's with that old letter *C* on it. And he was smiling that cocky smile that was so familiar to Sylvester.

"Eddie Cicotte," Sylvester murmured quietly, reading the name under the picture. "I just can't believe it."

"It really looks like this Cheeko guy?" asked Duane.

"*Exactly* like him," said Sylvester. "And he's a southpaw!"

As Sylvester shook his head in amazement, Duane stared at the ceiling.

"You know what I think?" Duane announced. "He's another look-alike. Just like Babe Ruth and that Mr. Baruth you mentioned. They're probably actors who do imitations of the Babe and Cheeko on stage or cable TV or something. And then they go on vacation to get away from all their fans, you know. So last year this Baruth guy picks this little hick town where nobody would probably recognize him. And he tells the guy playing Cheeko. Celebrities do things like that. Hey, they probably think they're just like the real thing and they can even play and coach and everything. Whatcha think?"

Sylvester didn't reply. Too much was going through his mind. Like, what about his hitting and fielding? How come he had gotten better so quickly? And not just a little better, but phenomenally better, like all those great catches and home runs.

"You think maybe it's some kind of ghost or something like in the movies?" asked Sylvester.

"Boy, wouldn't that be something!" said Duane.

"Wait a minute," Sylvester said. "I've got to tell my dad about this."

He went into the living room and saw that his father had nodded off in the comfortable padded chair. Sylvester knew it was just a nap and it wouldn't take much to arouse him.

"Ahem." He coughed, pretending not to notice

his father's closed eyelids. "Say, Dad, could you come and take a look at something weird?"

"Sure." Mr. Coddmyer yawned, rubbing his knuckles in his eyes. "Always interested in the oddball."

In the dining room, Sylvester showed him the two cards.

"Know these guys, Dad?" he asked.

His father picked up the cards and looked at the photos. "Babe Ruth and Eddie Cicotte," he said, smiling. "Sure, I remember them well."

"You do?" Sylvester stared at him. "But you weren't even born . . ."

"No," Mr. Coddmyer said with a chuckle, "but I've read about them. Ruth was the greatest, everyone knows that. Cicotte, now, he was one of the players involved in that Black Sox scandal."

"Sure, I've heard of them," said Duane. "But how'd they get that name, anyway?"

Mr. Coddmyer put down the cards. "It's the nickname they gave some bad apples on the 1919 Chicago White Sox team. Eight of them tried to fix the outcome of the World Series that year."

"Did they go to jail?" asked Duane.

"No, but they were banished from baseball. It was just about the worst scandal that ever happened to the game."

"Wow," said Sylvester. "I can't figure it out. Babe Ruth and Eddie Cicotte, they look exactly — I mean *exactly* — like Mr. Baruth and Cheeko, the two guys I told you about. You know, helping me out last year and now this year again."

"It could be a coincidence," said Mr. Coddmyer. "It could be some actors or impersonators . . ."

"That's what I said," Duane blurted out.

"But I'm not sure I buy that," Mr. Coddmyer continued.

Neither do I, Sylvester thought. How would that explain my improvement, my home runs?

He couldn't sluff it off with easy answers. Duane wanted to believe in impersonators and his father would settle for coincidence, but Sylvester wasn't convinced of either.

Mr. Coddmyer picked up a few of the other cards and commented about several of them. Sylvester was surprised that he knew so much about the old-timers. His father's job was keeping him so busy lately, they hadn't had much of a chance to shoot the breeze like this.

"Well, enjoy the cards, guys, and clean up when you're through," said Mr. Coddmyer. "I'm going to see what your mother finds so fascinating in her magazine, Sylvester."

He started to leave, then turned at the doorway, and said in what sounded like a casual voice, "By the way, Syl, that fellow you mentioned — Cheeko? Next time you're going to get together with him, let us know. I think your mother or I should meet him before you spend any more time with him. Okay?"

"Sure, Dad," Sylvester said.

Duane seemed to have lost interest in Cheeko by now and just wanted to go through the rest of his cards. Sylvester tried to pay attention but his mind wouldn't settle down. He kept sneaking glances at those two cards. There was no doubt that the resemblance was amazing.

After Duane left, Sylvester returned to the living room. His father was now wearing headphones to listen to a CD without disturbing Mrs. Coddmyer. She had her feet up on the sofa and was working away at a crossword puzzle.

"Mind if I watch TV?" he asked. His mother nodded silently. His father waved his hand, but Sylvester wasn't sure whether he was keeping time to the music or signaling to him.

He turned on the TV and clicked through the various channels. Just a bunch of reruns and talk shows. Even the sports channel had nothing but a boring old golf tournament in Japan! And it was Friday. He could stay up later since he didn't have to go to school the next day. He wondered what Joyce Dancer was doing. He wished he'd made some kind of plan to see her that evening, even if they just went for a walk.

Every now and then, Sylvester glanced over at his father. He wanted to ask him some questions about when he was a kid and how he knew so much about baseball. Did his father play Little League baseball? Or was he into football? Basketball? Hockey? Did *his* father come to many of his games? Did *his* father have time to play ball with him? Even a game of catch? It seemed that lately Mr. Coddmyer was always too busy working or too tired from work to spend much time with Sylvester.

"I think I'll go to bed," he said, getting up and stretching his arms.

His mother glanced at the clock on the mantel, then shot a surprised look at him. "It's not even nine o'clock yet," she observed. "Are you all right, Sylvester?"

"I'm fine," he said. "I guess I'm a little more tired from playing today than I realized. I'll read a little, then hit the sack."

"Good night, dear, and sleep well," his mother said.

He leaned over and gave his mother a kiss on the cheek and then did the same to his father, just grazing an earphone. He could hear violins and trumpets. Probably Beethoven or something like that, he thought.

He went up to his room, got undressed, and crawled into bed. He didn't even try to read; he knew he wouldn't be able to concentrate. There were too many things rolling around in his head.

Were Mr. Baruth and Cheeko ghosts? Actors? Or what had his mother said . . . angels? And how come they picked him to help out? His father didn't seem too worried, just curious. He wanted to meet Cheeko. Okay, he could meet him the next morning at practice. Would Cheeko be there? Would Sylvester keep hitting home runs and making great catches? How long would it last? Would it go on until the end of the season like last year? Would Cheeko disappear just like Mr. Baruth?

He had no idea how long he was awake, thinking all those thoughts, but the next thing he knew, there was bright sunshine streaming through his bedroom windows underneath the shades.

At breakfast, he was all set to ask his father to come watch him practice with Cheeko, but Mr. Coddmyer was nowhere in sight.

"Where's Dad?" he asked his mother.

"He took the lawn mower in for service so he could use it later this morning," she answered, sipping her black coffee. "I think he's counting on you to help him clean up the yard."

"Yeah, I can do that . . . later," Sylvester mumbled into his cereal. "Uh, Mom, are you busy right now?"

"I'm going to attack those hedges out back before they turn into the Great Wall of China," she announced firmly. "Somehow your father never manages to get around to it."

She got up and grabbed her gardening gloves, calling back as she left the kitchen, "Clean up your mess before you go anywhere, young man!"

Sylvester carefully washed his breakfast dishes and put them in the drying rack. It was after nine o'clock. Cheeko would be waiting for him at the park.

What had his father said? He wanted to meet Cheeko. Or he wanted Mrs. Coddmyer to meet Cheeko. He didn't exactly say Sylvester couldn't even see Cheeko until then, did he? At least, it hadn't sounded that way.

Sylvester ran to the park. He'd just hit a few or field a couple of Cheeko's hits. And he'd get a chance to ask Cheeko some things, like where he lived, and what he did. Was he an actor? And what did he know about that Eddie Cicotte?

But the park was empty. Not a soul in sight. Clean as a whistle, except for a piece of paper under a stone on the pitcher's mound.

He picked it up and read the message:

"Sorry, pal, can't make it. Got a few things to take care of. See you next game."

It was signed with the letter *C*.

He crumpled it up and dumped it into the trash bin on his way out of the park.

Well, at least he didn't have to lie to his folks about meeting Cheeko behind their backs, after all.

He got home in time to help his father unload the lawn mower. While Sylvester hauled away hedge clippings from out back, Mr. Coddmyer put the mower to good use in front.

Later on, after they put away the mower, Mr. Coddmyer grabbed a rake and handed another to Sylvester.

"Might as well get some of these clippings," he announced.

This was the chance Sylvester was looking for.

"Dad," he said, "did you ever play ball when you were a kid? You never told me."

"I never did? That's amazing. Yes, I played . . . Little League and in high school. After that I went off to college and had to work part time to help pay for it. College was expensive, even back then," Mr. Coddmyer explained.

"Were you a pretty good player?"

"I thought so — but I didn't have the opportunity to find out. Or maybe the drive. I loved playing, even on days when I didn't see much action. It was great just being out at the park, doing the best I could. That's all anyone can do."

"Did you ever go to any games? You know, pro games?"

"A few, not many." Mr. Coddmyer paused and leaned on his rake. "I sense something behind these questions, Syl. What's up?"

Sylvester stared at the grass pile on the ground in front of him and said softly, "I guess, well, I just wish we could spend more time together, Dad."

Mr. Coddmyer came over to him and put an arm around his shoulders. "I'm sorry your mother and I have been so busy lately, Syl," he said. "It's not deliberate, you know that. Just the same old excuse, I'm afraid. Too busy making a living, not enough hours in the day. The usual, I don't have to tell you, you've heard it enough."

He rubbed his knuckles on top of Sylvester's blond hair teasingly. "Hey, I'll tell you what. The next time the Chiefs play a weekend game, we'll make a day of it." Mr. Coddmyer was referring to the Syracuse Chiefs of the International League. They played local games in a neighboring town. "Just your mother, you, and me. A swim at the lake, picnic lunch, then hours of good baseball. What do you say?"

"Sure!"

"Good. Well, looks like we've got just a bit more work to do here, so let's get to it!"

After hurrying through the raking, Sylvester rushed inside to look at the paper to see when the Chief's next weekend game was to be played

"They're playing next Saturday, Dad. Do you really think Mom will be able to come along, too?"

"Come along? Where? Where are we going now?" Mrs. Coddmyer poked her head into the living room where they were looking at the paper. "I'm not going anywhere I have to look decent," she joked.

"Dad's taking us to see the Syracuse Chiefs play next Saturday. Do you have it free?" an excited Sylvester blurted out.

"Well," she considered, "I could stay home and wash my hair, balance my checkbook, look over some work . . . or go to a baseball game." She paused, then smiled and said, "Just don't expect me to be the only one preparing sandwiches for the picnic lunch!"

The thought of food reminded Sylvester that he hadn't had any lunch. While he was making himself a peanut butter and banana sandwich, Joyce Dancer called.

"There's a good movie playing at the Cineplex Theater, Syl," she said. "Want to go this afternoon?"

"Sure," he said. He didn't even ask her what the movie was. It made no difference to him. He was glad to have a chance to spend some time with her.

It was a silly cops-and-robbers movie, but they had a few laughs and held hands through most of it. Afterward, they went over to the local hangout and sat slurping milk shakes.

Joyce, still laughing over the dumb movie, started to talk about one of the funny scenes that had broken her up. But Sylvester barely heard what she was saying. He was thinking about Cheeko and wondering what he had had to do that was so important he missed practice.

After a couple of minutes, Joyce noticed he wasn't really listening. "What's the matter? I thought you liked the movie."

He forced a grin. "I did. I was just thinking about something else, that's all."

Joyce shrugged. "Oh, well, I guess I'm not as interesting as a certain guy named Cheeko."

He had a mouthful of milk shake halfway down his throat and, as he gagged, it almost came up out of his nose. Luckily, he managed to swallow it before gasping out, "How do you know about him?"

"Duane told me."

"Duane! What did he say?"

Joyce stirred her straw around the glass. "Nothing much, except you think he's terrific since he's helping you play better baseball. Maybe even a little *dirty* baseball."

"Dirty?"

"Yes, Syl, dirty. What else do you call that cheap shot you took at Russ Skelton yesterday?"

"It wasn't a cheap shot," he insisted. "Anyhow,

Duane's been shooting off his mouth too much. Oh, look who just came in — that great fortune-teller, Snooky Malone."

"Who's that behind him?"

"A couple of guys on the Macon Falcons."

He looked past her shoulder at the three of them making their way down the aisle, Snooky leading the way. Duke Farrell, tall and bushy-haired, followed with an arrogant swagger. Steve Button was an inch shorter; he was broad-shouldered and wore a crew cut.

"Hey Joyce! Hey Sylvester!" Snooky exclaimed when he caught sight of them. He stopped directly in front of their booth, blocking the aisle. "How'd you like the movie?"

"You were at the movies?" Joyce asked, looking past him to the burly boys who were waiting impatiently behind Snooky.

"Uh-huh." Snooky nodded. "Mind if I join you?"

Before Sylvester or Joyce could say a word, Snooky slid into the seat next to her. Duke and Steve shot a dirty look in Syl's direction, then climbed into the booth next to theirs.

"That's the dude everybody's talking about," Duke

said loudly. "The kid who hit all those homers last year and finally got a few measly hits this year."

"Yeah, but ya'see, Syl-vest-er only hits 'em this year with men on base," Steve drawled. "Makes you wonder, doesn't it?"

Duke snorted. "Well, I'll tell you one thing, when we play those Redbirds on Tuesday, he ain't even going to *see* that ball, because I'm pitching. So forget about home runs, Syl-ves-ter." He drawled out the name just as his pal had.

"You know who's going to hit that ball, don't you?" Steve flexed his biceps. He was sure everyone knew he was leading the league with an average close to .425.

Sylvester wheeled around in his seat and started to retort. His blood was simmering by now, but Joyce looked even angrier. She grabbed her purse and shoved Snooky out of the booth. She faced Duke and Steve, her eyes flashing.

"If you guys think I'm going to sit here and listen to this all afternoon, guess again. I have better things to do with my Saturday!" she snapped at them. "And as for you, Sylvester, don't bother to call me until you're able to concentrate on something other than baseball, or ghosts, or planning your next cheap shot at another player, or whatever it is you're so distracted by lately!"

She stalked out of the restaurant, ignoring Duke and Steve's laughter. "Move, Snooky!" Sylvester shouted, pushing his friend out of the way.

"See you on Tuesday, Syl-vest-er!" Duke sang after him. "And be ready for a row of 0's on the scoreboard, under Hooper Redbirds!"

"We'll just see about that," Sylvester muttered. "We'll just see."

Outside, there was no sign of Joyce.

"Rats!" he snarled, kicking his sneaker against a rock. "A lot she cares about me. Well, too bad for her if she's not interested. I'm not giving up baseball just for some girl."

But somehow or other, he just didn't feel so good as he slowly walked down the street in the direction of his home.

12

The game on Tuesday afternoon was played at the Macon Falcons' athletic field. As the Hooper Redbirds rode there on a chartered bus, next Saturday night's Chiefs game ran through Sylvester's mind. He could almost imagine himself wearing a Chiefs uniform, playing under the lights on the bright green field.

The bus pulled in at three o'clock, in just enough time for the team to change into uniforms and practice before the game started at four.

As they left the locker room and ran out to the field, Sylvester saw Duke Farrell warming up with his catcher, Greg Jackson. A mocking grin came over the cocky pitcher's face. Smile now, pal, Sylvester thought, because you'll wear a different expression when I'm up at bat.

As soon as that thought occurred, he started to have misgivings. Suppose Duke does strike me out every time I'm up? It could happen. The whole Falcon team, the whole park, everyone would laugh me off the field.

Especially Trent Sturgis. The Hooper team's ace slugger this season hadn't been hitting all that well lately and seemed to be nursing a grudge against Sylvester.

The Redbirds were up first. Jim Cowley, at the top of the batting order, fouled off two pitches, then let four balls go by to earn himself a walk. Hmm, maybe that smartmouth Farrell isn't as hot as he pretends, Sylvester mused.

But then Ted Sobel went down in three, and Trent hit a weak grounder to short, almost resulting in a double play. Jim was out at second, but the combination of the slow bouncing ball and Trent's speed put him safely at first.

Sylvester was up next. He let out a deep breath as he left the on-deck circle and walked to the plate, wondering what would happen. He was nervous, but he couldn't let Duke see that. Stare 'im down, that's what Cheeko would do.

Swish! The pitch streaked past Sylvester's stomach for a ball. If he hadn't moved, he would have been hit. Maybe he should lean into an easy one and fake being hit, just as Cheeko had taught him. He shuddered at the thought.

"Ball two!" Again Duke zipped the ball inside the plate, forcing Sylvester to jump back several inches to avoid being hit.

He stepped out of the box, rubbed his gloved hands up and down the bat, took another deep breath, exhaled, then stepped back into the box. Sylvester fixed a hard, determined glare on the Falcons' hurler as he wound up for his next pitch.

"Strike!" yelled the ump as the ball just grazed the inside of the plate.

It seems as though Duke saved his best stuff for me, Sylvester thought. No easy pickin's here.

"Ball three!"

Again the ball came threateningly close, forcing Sylvester practically to fall back from the plate. Thinking again of Cheeko's lesson, he pondered letting one of them hit him. It would be a sure way of ending the tension.

He took off his batting helmet and wiped his

brow, glancing into the stands. He was happy to see Cheeko at the near end of the first base line. But Cheeko wasn't looking back at him. His eyes were fixed, almost a glassy stare, right at the mound.

Sweat made Sylvester's vision a little blurry, but for one second, he thought he saw a sort of round, familiar face, frowning at him from high up in the stands. At a distance, it looked a little like . . . like Mr. Baruth. But then the man looked down and he couldn't really tell. Sylvester shook his head and put his helmet back on.

Duke's next pitch looked as though it was going to be high and inside, the toughest spot for Sylvester to hit. But it seemed to curve at the last second and slide right down the middle. He swung at it with all his might.

Crack! It was a solid blow. Sylvester knew the instant his bat connected with the ball that it was a goner. He'd felt that same sensation before and each time it was an over-the-fence wallop.

He watched the ball sail out to deep left field as he started to run, dropping his bat a third of the way down the base line. The Redbirds' fans cheered and whistled. He felt like doffing his hat to them as he rounded the bases, but he knew better than to show off. Getting a home run and bringing in a man on base was enough.

Again he was greeted at the plate by his happy teammates. All, that is, except Trent, who mixed in with the gang at the plate — but didn't even make a show of holding out his hand.

Stick it in your nose, Trent, Sylvester thought.

"Nice blast, Syl," said his buddy Duane.

Sylvester shrugged. "Thanks, pal," he said. "Now it's your turn."

But Duane, up next, popped out to first base. Three outs.

Hooper Redbirds 2, Macon Falcons 0.

By now, Sylvester was relaxed enough to check out the crowd as he ran off to his position in right field. There, of course, was Cheeko. He actually wasn't too far from where the man who looked like Mr. Baruth had been sitting. Only that seat was now empty.

Apparently, neither his mother nor his father had made the game. Too busy with work. Oh, well, he couldn't complain too much since they were all going to the Chief's game this weekend.

But where was Joyce? He knew another busload of Hooper fans had followed the team. Maybe she had given up on him.

Ray Bottoms, the Falcons' shortstop, led off and pounded Terry Barnes's second pitch for a hard, shallow drive between Bobby and Sylvester for a double. This time the Falcons' fans, who outnumbered the Redbirds' fans about four to one, applauded.

Left fielder Kirk Anderson walloped a fastball down to short, which Trent scooped up and pegged to first for an out. But the next batter, Ernie Fantelli, came through with another double to score Ray.

"C'mon, Terry! C'mon, kid! Let's get 'em outta there!" Sylvester chimed in with the rest of the team on the field.

The cleanup hitter was Steve Button, the other unwelcome visitor who had butted in on Sylvester and Joyce after the movies. He took two hefty swings at Terry's fastball, then drove one a mile high toward the right center fence. No doubt about it — it was Sylvester's ball. He was after it, running sideways toward the fence, the second he saw it arcing in his direction.

As he neared the fence, he could tell that the ball

would clear it only by inches unless he could leap high enough to make the grab.

It was almost impossible, but he tried. As he pushed off with all his might, he felt a rush underneath him, like a springboard shoved under his feet. He rose into the air and . . . plop! The ball smacked in the pocket of his glove and stuck there.

His feet landed back on earth and he quickly pegged the ball to second. Jim caught it and whipped it to third, but not in time to nab Ernie as he slid safely into the bag.

Again, there was a wild ovation from the Redbirds' fans for Sylvester's sensational catch. There was an ear-to-ear smile on Cheeko's face as he clapped along with the crowd.

Sylvester felt incredibly good. That catch ought to take a little wind out of Button's overblown ego, he thought.

Scuttling into position for the next batter, he shouted, "One more to go, Terry! Only one more!"

Robbie Axelrod, the Falcons' short, well-built third baseman, connected with a low, inside pitch that struck the left field fence for a triple, scoring Ernie. And then Tom Stringer struck out.

Redbirds 2, Falcons 2.

"Okay, Bobby, break the tie," shouted Coach Corbin. "Nail that ball!"

Bobby Kent, leading off at the top of the second inning for the Redbirds, did nail Duke's first pitch over second base for a single.

As Jerry Ash, the next batter, headed for the plate, Sylvester heard a familiar voice at a familiar spot — his elbow. "You did it again, Syl. You can do it every time you want to, can't you?"

Snooky Malone was at his side again. His face was wreathed in a broad smile.

"Do what? Who cares? Oh, never mind!" Sylvester snapped before Snooky had a chance to answer. "Buzz off, will you? What are you doing here, anyway?"

Snooky's cheerful expression faded. His face got all flushed. "Sorry, Syl," he said, apologetically. "I didn't mean to bother you. After all, I'm your friend, not your enemy."

Without another word, he stepped out of the dugout, never looking back.

Sylvester sat there, fuming. The little creep, he thought, he really sounded sorry. Maybe he was. But

I don't have to sit there and take it every time he needles me, do I? I can give it as well as take it. That's what Cheeko would expect from me now.

Yeah, Cheeko had shown him a thing or two. And it was starting to pay off. He had to play tough . . . and be tough, no matter what. Well, that's what he'd do from now on, even with the likes of Snooky Malone.

"What was all that about?" Duane asked, sliding into the vacant space next to his friend.

"Nothing. Just a lot of nothing," Sylvester answered.

He fixed his attention at the plate in time to see Jerry Ash lay down a bunt, sending Bobby safely to second, but getting thrown out himself.

"Bring 'im home, Eddie!" Sylvester shouted as the Redbirds' catcher stepped up to the plate, pulling on his batting gloves.

Eddie did, with a long triple to right center field. Then Terry fanned, and Jim singled, scoring Eddie. With the one man on, Ted popped up to third, ending the half inning.

Terry held the Falcons to a walk in the bottom of the inning, so no runs scored.

The Redbirds came up again with Trent leading off. His slump continued as he struck out.

Sylvester couldn't help but grin as he passed Trent on his way to the batter's box amidst loud cheers and applause from the stands.

With a cocky stance, he ground his feet into the dirt and took the first pitch — a called strike that seemed a little inside to him, almost a brush.

The next pitch did more than brush him. It hit him.

13

Base!" yelled the ump. Then, to Duke, "Watch it, Farrell. You're putting some of 'em awfully close in there, mister. Another one like that, and you're outta here!"

About time, thought Sylvester. Boy, that sure hurt. It never felt like that when he practiced with Cheeko, when they weren't for real.

Sylvester rubbed the bruised spot where the ball had hit. His side throbbed, but he wasn't about to let anyone know how much it hurt. After all, he had brought it on himself, by leaning into the pitch slightly. And you had to act tough, he remembered.

The next batter, Duane, cracked a single over shortstop, advancing Sylvester to second base. But neither of them got any farther. Bobby hit a line drive to the shortstop, and Jerry fanned. Three out.

As Sylvester ran to the dugout for his glove, Coach Corbin looked worried.

"Are you okay?" he asked.

"Sure, coach," Sylvester replied. "I can hardly feel it any more." But I won't forget it, he added to himself.

Ray Bottoms led off for the Falcons and lined a three-one pitch directly to Trent for the first out. Kirk Anderson fared no better, popping the first pitch back to Terry.

"One more, Terry! One-two-three!" shouted Sylvester as Ernie Fantelli stepped up to the plate.

But Terry pitched four balls, none of which crossed the plate, and Ernie had a free ticket to first base.

With little happening in the outfield, Sylvester looked around the stands and caught Cheeko's eye. Leaning back in his seat, Cheeko made a little jab with his fist that looked like a cross between an okay sign and thumbs-up. Sylvester gave him a quick wave and turned back to the action on the field.

Cleanup slugger Steve Button had just stepped to

the plate and all three outfielders edged themselves back a little. Steve was ready and walloped Terry's first pitch out toward center field. It looked as if it was all Bobby's, an easy out. But just as the ball started its downward arc, Bobby tripped as though he'd stumbled into something.

It seemed miles away, but Sylvester had to try for it. From out of nowhere, he felt a rush of energy as he made his move. With lightning speed, he crossed into the center field zone, put out his glove, and grabbed the ball just inches from the turf.

There was a thunderous ovation as the Redbirds came off the field. Sylvester could hear his name being called in the midst of all the shouting.

Flopping down onto the bench, Bobby shook his head as he tried to explain what happened.

"Like, it was weird," he said. "It felt like somone pulled the ground out from under my foot."

"Maybe it was a ghost." Ted Sobel offered this with a laugh.

Sylvester felt a little lump in his throat.

The Hooper team went down in three as they came to bat in the top of the fourth inning. In the bottom, Robbie Axelrod led off for the Falcons and made the game interesting by blasting a home run over the left field fence.

Tom Stringer kept things rolling by smashing a hard grounder down toward the shortstop position. It looked as if Trent had it, but it went through his legs for an error.

Get your tailgate down, Big Shot, Sylvester felt like yelling at him — but knew enough not to.

Ed Norman flied out to center field, but Greg Jackson smacked a triple along the third base line. That scored Tom and brought up the smartmouth pitcher, Duke Farrell.

Two runs, one out, and a man was on third.

Sylvester joined in with his teammates, shouting toward the mound, "Hold 'em, Terry! You can do it!"

But Duke slashed a single by the pitcher to score Greg and put the Falcons ahead by one run.

Coach Corbin ran out of the dugout as the umpire raised his hands for a time out.

The coach talked with Terry for a moment, then took the ball from the downcast pitcher. He waved in Rick Wilson, who had been warming up in front of the first base seats.

After a few warm-up throws, the game resumed.

Rick managed to hold Ray Bottoms to a groundout to second, and Kirk Anderson to a pop fly to first base. Three out. Redbirds 4, Falcons 5.

Ted led off in the top of the fifth with a single through the gap between first and second bases. Trent, up next, lined one over short, advancing Ted to second.

Sylvester stepped into the batter's box. A big cheer rose up from the Redbirds' fans as he thumped the fat end of his bat against the plate and waited for the pitch.

As he stared down the pitcher, he tried to forget the sensation of being hit by the ball last time. Instead, he checked out his stance, his grip, and each pitch as it came toward him.

"Strike!"

It was inside, just grazing the plate.

"Strike two!" The second pitch was almost in the very same spot.

Then, "Ball!" Yes, but it just missed the plate by an inch. Duke was in his absolute best form.

Then, crack! Sylvester swung, connected, and drove the ball toward deep center field. It cleared the fence by five feet and cleaned the bases for three runs.

The ovation was deafening as Sylvester dropped his bat and circled the bases.

His teammates greeted him with high fives as he crossed the plate — again, all but Trent, who hung back. And, as he headed for the dugout, there was Snooky Malone jumping up and down.

"I can't help it, Sylvester," said Snooky, his voice hoarse from cheering. "You came through, just as I knew you could — and would."

Sylvester barely slapped Snooky's extended hand before he turned away. But I have to admit that the little guy sure had guts to come over and congratulate me, after the way I've been treating him. Maybe I ought to take it easy on him, he considered.

But Snooky had vanished. Sylvester removed his batting gloves, pushed them into his pocket, and settled down in the dugout.

This game is going so great, he thought. I hope my folks are out there somewhere. Mom said she was going to try to get someone to cover for her at work. Maybe she got here in time for that home run. But I don't suppose I'd be lucky enough for Dad to go without a call on his beeper this afternoon.

Duane Francis batted a double, his second hit of the game. But Duke mowed down the next three batters and the half inning was over. Redbirds 7, Falcons 5.

The Falcons put one man on base during their turn at bat. Steve Button had fouled off three pitches. It looked as if Rick was starting to lose control and then he walked him. The next three batters went down in a row and that was it.

A caught pop fly, a single, and then a double play in the sixth and last inning ended the Redbirds' chances of collecting any more runs.

Two singles and two walks resulted in another run for the Falcons in the bottom of the inning but that was all the scoring that took place. When the game ended, it was Redbirds 7, Falcons 6.

At the final out, an ovation resounded in the stands as the crowd swarmed down onto the field. In no time, Sylvester found himself surrounded by friends, admirers, and for the first time this season, newspaper reporters. He recognized a few faces, from the *Hooper Herald* and the *Chronicle*. They had both sent writers out to cover the game.

"Sylvester," began the reporter from the *Herald,* "I've noticed something unusual about your hitting this year. You've never gotten a hit when the bases were empty. And, when there was someone on base, you not only got a hit, it was always a home run. Any way you can explain that, well, that phenomenon?"

"Phenomenon? No, I guess I can't," replied Sylvester, honestly.

"Do you do anything different, or feel anything different, when you're in those situations?" asked the reporter for the *Chronicle*.

"I don't know. I don't think so," Sylvester mumbled. Maybe it was just coincidence, Sylvester wanted to say. Deep down, though, he wondered if it was something else. Something called Cheeko.

The reporters kept up their barrage of questions. Syl heard the steady click of cameras snapping and the whir of camcorders getting it all on tape. He looked around to see if he could find someone else to talk to. Where was Joyce? Had she come to the game? And what about his mother and father? They were nowhere in sight.

"What about your fielding, Sylvester?" continued the woman from the *Herald*, waving a microphone toward Syl's face. He tried to push away the memory of the force he had felt propelling him into the air — and the one that had tripped up Bobby.

"Sorry," he said, his nerves getting on edge. "I have to go now." Same as last year, he thought, same big hullabaloo. It was sort of fun back then, but now . . . it doesn't seem so much like I deserve all this attention.

"Would you be surprised if a few years from now some major league team offered you a contract?" the reporter for the *Herald* persisted.

"No, I wouldn't be surprised!" Sylvester finally snapped. "Why? Because in a few years I will be good enough to play in the majors!" With that, he pushed past the surprised woman and climbed aboard the waiting bus.

He was sure he'd told them what Cheeko would have expected him to say. He wasn't sure it came out sounding so good, though.

The bus unloaded its passengers back at the

school, across from the field. Before heading home, Sylvester strolled over to the bleachers and sat down. It was nearly dark, and he hadn't noticed one occupied seat at the far end. After a few minutes, he heard a voice come from that direction.

"I just don't know what to think of you now, Sylvester. I just don't know."

It couldn't be.

Sylvester got up and climbed over the bleachers. It was Mr. Baruth!

"Mr. Baruth! What are you doing here? When did you get back?" he asked, the words pouring out in his excitement.

"That doesn't matter," said Mr. Baruth. "I don't have time to go into all that right now. Maybe someday. What's important is what has happened to you."

"What do you mean?" asked Sylvester, chewing on his lower lip.

"Last year, I tried to help you become a better player because I saw a lot of potential there. Sort of a chip off an old block that never really got a chance."

I bet he's talking about Dad, Sylvester thought.

"And, just as important, you were a good, honest kid," Mr. Baruth went on.

"I . . . I still am," Sylvester stammered.

"Are you? Can you honestly tell me you aren't cutting corners, shaving around the edges, so to speak?"

"But . . . but Cheeko says . . ."

"Cheeko! Who cares what he says?" Mr. Baruth snapped.

"Isn't he a friend of yours? He says he knows you," Sylvester insisted.

"Knowing someone doesn't make that person your friend," said Mr. Baruth. "And it doesn't matter how someone else tells you to play the game. You're old enough to know what's right and wrong yourself. You shouldn't need any outside help."

"But what will happen if . . . if . . . ?"

"If you just play clean, the way you learned from Coach Corbin and from my few suggestions last year? Well, Sylvester, there's only one way you'll ever know."

Sylvester stared down at his shoes, his eyes smarting and the back of his throat all choked up.

When he lifted his head, Mr. Baruth was gone.

14

"Hello, Joyce? It's Syl," he spoke into the telephone. "I didn't see you after the game today. What? Oh . . . well, maybe I'll talk to you later."

So she hadn't been at the game. It made her too uncomfortable to see him turning into such a bully. He couldn't even defend himself when she said that.

"I got that book you asked about," his mother called from the dining room. After dinner she liked to sit there drinking her coffee and reading the newspaper while his father carried on a commentary about the silly letters to the editor.

"Thanks, Mom," he said as he took the book up to his room. It was a history of the World Series from the very first to the one played just last year. He quickly turned to the section on 1919.

There it was, all about the Black Sox scandal.

Eddie Cicotte, the pitcher, was right in there with seven others who were accused of fixing the outcome of the series by the way they hit and fielded — or didn't hit and committed fake errors. The author claimed that they had had a score to settle with the team's owners, who had treated them badly.

I don't have any score to settle with anyone, thought Sylvester. Even when I wasn't playing so hot, Coach Corbin treated me like any other player. It was my own fault, if anything, that I was in a slump.

There was a picture of the team and he picked out Eddie Cicotte. He looked just as he did on the card Duane had lent him; he'd had to promise Duane he'd guard it with his life since it was sort of rare.

It was still light out. Sylvester remembered what his father had said about wanting to meet Cheeko, but that was when he was going to practice with him. Maybe it would be okay if he just went for a walk in the direction of the field while it was still light out.

He hadn't gotten three blocks from his house when he saw Cheeko coming toward him.

"Hi, Cheeko," Sylvester said, not that surprised to bump into him.

"Hi, Syl," said Cheeko. "What brings you out this time of day, or should I say night? You should be celebrating after the way you played today."

"Right," said Sylvester, "but first I want to show you this."

He reached into his pocket and brought out a baseball card.

"I borrowed it from my friend Duane, you know, our third baseman?" he said. He handed it to Cheeko, who examined it closely.

"Hey, how about that?" Cheeko cried out with gusto. "Eddie Cicotte! Chicago White Sox!"

"Then you know him?" Sylvester asked, searching Cheeko's eyes and face.

"Know him? Who doesn't?" Cheeko replied. "Everybody who knows anything about baseball has heard of him. Well, almost everybody."

There were so many questions in Sylvester's mind, he didn't know which to ask first. But he knew that he had to get some answers or they would haunt him forever.

"That picture . . . uh . . . it sort of . . . well, doesn't it," he hemmed and hawed, "doesn't it look a little . . . ?"

"Like me?" Cheeko finished, his grin spreading wider than ever.

"Yeah!" Sylvester shouted, relieved.

"Well, I'd be lying if I said that it doesn't, 'cause it does, doesn't it?"

"Sure does," nodded Sylvester.

"Look, you can walk down the street and see someone who looks like the president of the United States," Cheeko continued, "but that doesn't mean this guy is the president of the United States, does it?"

"No, but . . ."

"Syl, let me tell you something. There're a lot of coincidences and a lot of strange things in this world. Don't expect answers for everything."

He handed back the card and threw back his shoulders, the way he always did when he was all through practice and ready to leave.

"Are . . . are you going somewhere now?" Sylvester asked.

"It's near the end of the line for us, kid," Cheeko said, looking around.

"But I still have a lot of questions I have to ask you," Sylvester said.

"I'm a little short on answers, right now," Cheeko said abruptly. "Tell you what, I'll see you at the game next week. We'll talk afterward."

Before Sylvester could get another word out, Cheeko had turned, raced across the street, and was out of sight in an instant.

But what about Mr. Baruth? What about what he said about your not being friends? What about the Black Sox scandal?

And what about some of the strange things that kept happening at games? Bobby tripping over nothing? A pitch taking a weird turn so he could hit it? A miraculous boost so he could grab a ball going over the fence?

And, craziest of all, this business of him only hitting home runs when there were men on base?

Were those things all coincidences?

"Rats!" he shouted out loud in frustration. Would he ever get to find out?

"Sylvester!"

He whirled around. It was Snooky Malone.

"What are you doing here, Snooky? You don't live on this street."

"That's what I was going to ask you," said Snooky.

"I come around the corner and there you are, standing like you're in a trance or something, and then yelling at nothing. Are you okay?"

"I'm fine, just fine," replied Sylvester.

He glanced across the street. No, Cheeko wasn't coming back.

"Looking for somebody?" Snooky asked.

"Nope."

He realized he still had the baseball card in his hand and started to put it back into his jacket pocket.

"What's that?" Snooky asked.

"Just one of Duane's baseball cards," said Sylvester, trying to shrug off the question.

"Can I see it? Please?"

What difference could it make? Sylvester paused, heaved a deep sigh, and said, "Okay, but don't take all night. I have to be home before the streetlights go on."

He handed Snooky the card.

"Eddie Cicotte," Snooky read. He turned it over. "Chicago White Sox. A southpaw. Hmmmm . . . never heard of him." He returned the card to Sylvester. "Why are you carrying his card?"

Sylvester shook his head. "No reason in particular," he said. "Duane, uh, left it at my house the other night. It's very valuable because Eddie Cicotte was a famous player."

"He couldn't be all that famous," Snooky said. "Like I told you, I never heard of him."

Sylvester took back the card and put it in his pocket.

"You know something, Snooky, there's a lot of things you never heard of. So don't expect answers for everything, okay?"

15

Sylvester was late leaving the locker room for the start of the game with the Broton Tigers. In fact, it had just about cleared out when he saw Cheeko standing in the doorway.

"Hey, buddy," said Cheeko, with his usual grin. "All set for the big one, huh?"

A win over the Tigers would guarantee the Redbirds a shot at the league championship.

"Yeah, and I'd better get out there with the guys to warm up," Sylvester replied. Too bad there wasn't time right now to ask Cheeko any of the questions that had been running through his brain for days.

"Right," agreed Cheeko. "Just don't forget what I've been telling you. You can hit the ball and make the plays out in the field, even if it takes a little help now and then . . ."

"What do you mean?" asked Sylvester, almost afraid of what the answer might be.

"Never mind," Cheeko continued. "Just do what I taught you and don't be afraid to get tough. Don't let anybody walk all over you. Play hard, even a little 'tricky,' you know? Yeah, I know you do! I've seen everything you've done out there." He chuckled. "Hey, you dropped your glove."

Sylvester automatically bent down to pick up his glove. When he straightened up, Cheeko was gone.

His stomach fluttered around and around as he left the cool locker room for the warm field.

"Hey, you want to throw a few?" asked Bobby Kent as Sylvester walked by him. The last few games, Bobby had acted much friendlier. It was hard to believe that they used to be so mean to each other.

"Yeah, sure," said Sylvester, glumly.

They threw the ball back and forth a few times near the first base line. Sylvester's throws were so soft that twice they barely reached Bobby.

"Hey, Syl," Bobby called. "You okay?"

"Sure, sure, I'm fine."

"You don't act it," Bobby said. "Don't look it, either."

"I'm all right," Sylvester insisted.

Bobby pegged a stinger at him. It hit the tip of his glove and bounced into the seats next to first base. Sylvester went over to retrieve it from the fan who'd reached up and grabbed the ball with a practiced flair.

It was Mr. Baruth.

"Mr. Baruth!" he exclaimed. "Boy, am I glad to see you!"

"Hi, Sylvester," said Mr. Baruth. "I'm glad I could make this game. Hope it isn't too late."

"Too late? For what?"

"To put into practice some of the things I taught you."

"About my batting? And my fielding?"

"That's part of it." Mr. Baruth smiled.

Sylvester dropped his voice. "I guess you mean, like my attitude. Like what Cheeko taught me this year."

"Cheeko may have given you some pointers that have helped improve your game, but he overlooked the most important piece of advice he could have given you. Be true to yourself, Sylvester. Play the best you can but play clean and honest. You don't win any medals — or anything else — by playing dirty."

"But Mr. Baruth, didn't you, well, give me more

130

than advice last year? Didn't you give me some extra help? That's playing dirty, too, isn't it?" Sylvester felt awkward asking him straight out like this, but the thought had been nagging at him for a while, and he was glad he had finally said something.

Mr. Baruth looked straight into Sylvester's questioning eyes and said calmly, "The only thing I did was help you realize your potential."

"Hey, Sylvester! Game's starting!" shouted Bobby. "Come on!"

Sylvester didn't have time to digest Mr. Baruth's words as he took the ball from him, tossed it toward the pitcher's mound, and trotted out to right field. Advice from Cheeko, advice from Mr. Baruth, advice from the coach, from his father, Snooky, everyone. There were almost too many words of advice to fit under his cap.

The Broton Tigers, looking sharp in their orange uniforms, were up first. Right-hander Rick Wilson, hurling for the Hooper Redbirds, had no trouble disposing of the initial two batters, Chuck Manning and "Oink" Santos.

Then Steve Cranshaw came up blasted a triple to deep center field.

Get 'im outta there, Rick!" Sylvester shouted as Mike Hennesey, the cleanup hitter, stepped to the plate.

Mike was short, hefty, and batted left-handed. He fouled off the first pitch, took two balls, fouled off another, then took two more balls and walked.

"C'mon, Rick! You can do it!" Sylvester yelled, his voice mixing in with the other calls from his teammates.

Lennie Chang was the Tigers' fifth batter. He took two strikes, then sent the third pitch a mile high into the stratosphere. He was crossing first base when the ball descended and landed in third baseman Duane Francis's glove.

Three out.

"Okay! Cowley! Sobel! Sturgis!" scorekeeper Billy Haywood's clarion voice rang out.

Cowley, Sobel, and Sturgis, however, did nothing to help the cause. Jim struck out, Ted flied out to left field, and Trent popped up to the pitcher, flinging his bat toward the dugout with angry disgust.

"Creep!" muttered Sylvester to himself. "Keep acting like that and you'll never get a hit."

He was surprised by his own thought. Trent acted

tough, real mean, and it didn't do *him* any good. How come it worked for me? Is it because I'm getting "outside help"? I wish I could just forget about all this crazy stuff and play ball!

He tossed aside the bat he'd been holding in the on-deck circle, took off his batting gloves and helmet, and ran out to his spot in right field. When the Redbirds came up again, he'd be the leadoff batter. But that was something to think about later, not now.

B. K. Abbot, wearing a stubble of a mustache above his lip that made him look older than the rest of his teammates, led off the top of the second inning for the Tigers and belted a single over second baseman Jim Cowley's outstretched gloved hand. He missed it by just about an inch.

Gary Hutton walked, advancing B. K. to second, and Josh Nichols popped out to Duane. Jim Smith, up next, and batting left-handed, uncorked a shallow drive over first base that stayed in fair territory, then bounced out against the foul line beyond the first base bleachers.

Sylvester tore after it, scooped it up near the fence, and pegged it in to Jim Cowley.

But, by now, B. K. and Gary had scored, and Jim was safely on second base for a double.

From opposite sides of the first base seats, Sylvester could see two distinct faces, both smiling. Mr. Baruth was at one end and Cheeko at the other. It sure didn't look like they were friends.

"Nice peg, Syl," came Cheeko's voice. "Pace yourself, pal."

Mr. Baruth just beamed and said nothing.

Chuck Manning was up again. This time he drove one of Rick's fastballs through the hole between shortstop and third, scoring Jim. "Oink" Santos bounced one to shortstop, and Chuck got tapped out on the first step of a possible double play. Only his slide, going into the base directly in Jim Cowley's path, prevented the second baseman from making the play to first.

Steve Cranshaw grounded out to short, and the half inning was over. But it was a big half inning, and Sylvester wondered whether it was going to be the one that made the difference when it was over.

"Coddmyer! Francis! Kent!" shouted Billy Haywood as the Redbirds came in to start the bottom half of the inning.

Sylvester put on his gloves and helmet, picked out his favorite bat, and swung it from one shoulder to the other as he headed for the plate.

"Okay, Sylvester!" Coach Corbin shouted from the third base coaching box. "Start it off! You know what to do, kid!"

Sylvester looked over at the coach and caught a glimpse of the fans in the seats behind him. There were two people shouting and waving who really stood out — his mother and father. Mr. Coddmyer was giving him the high sign while Mrs. Coddmyer put her fingers to her lips and blew him a big kiss. And there, a few seats behind them, was Joyce. So she was willing to give him another chance.

He felt great. It was so good seeing all of them.

Swish! "Strike!" yelled the ump as Jim Smith breezed the first pitch past him.

He'd been wondering whether Joyce had come to the game. He hadn't really had a chance to check out the crowd until then.

"Strike two!" cried the ump.

Sylvester stepped out of the batting box, rubbed his gloved hands up and down the handle of the bat, and stepped in again. Two strikes, huh? Smith would probably waste the next one.

He didn't. It was right down the middle.

Sylvester swung and froze as the pitch landed kerthunk in the catcher's mitt.

The Redbirds' fans groaned. The Tigers' fans cheered.

"That's okay, Syl," said Duane as he passed by Sylvester on his way to the plate. "You'll get another shot."

But a strikeout? Sylvester kept his head bowed all the way to the dugout.

What was wrong with him? There was probably an easy answer if he could just concentrate. That was it! He hadn't been concentrating. He'd let his mind wander and that was the only reason he struck out. He didn't have to hit them all out of the park, but he did have to pay attention if he was going to get anywhere.

Now that's a real lesson, he thought as he put his mind to what was happening at the plate.

Duane had let the first two pitches go by, then

connected with a high one that he knocked to right center field for a double. Then Bobby Kent belted a line drive through the gap between first and second for a single, scoring Duane.

Jerry Ash and Eddie Exton could do nothing, and the inning was over. Broton Tigers 3, Hooper Redbirds 1.

Sylvester scooped up his glove and trotted out to right field. He tried to avoid Cheeko by not looking directly at him, but his glance swept in that area of the stands. There was Cheeko, standing next to Mr. Baruth. It looked as though they were arguing. At least, Cheeko seemed to be angry about something. Mr. Baruth just stood there, shaking his head.

As the fans got settled down for the next play, Sylvester set his mind to the action at the plate. Left-handed batter Mike Hennesey led off with a high fly to Jerry for the first out. Rick fanned Lennie Chang, walked B. K. Abbot with four straight pitches, then fanned Gary Hutton. Three out.

Rick himself led off the bottom of the third for the Redbirds, and Sylvester wondered if he'd have a chance to bat. He was fifth in the rotation.

Considering the success Jim Smith was having on the mound, his chances were slim.

They became even slimmer as Rick bounced out to shortstop.

Then the top of the batting order was up again, and Jim Cowley started some action with a single over short. Ted Sobel lambasted one to left field that looked as if it might go over the fence. It didn't, but it struck that barrier and bounced back. The Tigers' Gary Hutton grabbed it and pegged it in. The throw held Jim on third and Ted on second with a double.

Well, there sure are men on base now. If they're still on when I bat, what will I do? Sylvester felt a weak tremor inside him. Will I hit a home run? Or will I strike out again?

Trent waited out the count, walked, and now the bases were loaded.

Sylvester got up from his crouch in the on-deck circle.

Cheers exploded from the Redbirds' fans as he stepped to the plate, pulled down on his helmet, and waited for Jim Smith to pitch to him.

Then, for a long moment, the crowd was silent, so silent Sylvester could hear the pounding of his heart.

16

He tried to concentrate. What difference did it make whether it was a strikeout or a home run, as long as he did the best he could? That rang a bell! That's what his dad had said, and what Mr. Baruth had always told him. And Coach Corbin. Even Joyce said so. In fact, the only one who had never said that was Cheeko!

Jim Smith's first three pitches were all curves, none of which went over the plate.

Then he blazed in a fastball. "Strike!" called the ump as Sylvester let it go by.

The next pitch was a fastball, too, but this one was grazing the outside corner when Sylvester's bat connected with it. The sound was like a rifle shot, and the ball like a white bullet as it streaked out to deep left center field . . . and over the fence.

The crowd was on its feet as the applause echoed and reechoed throughout the park. Sylvester dropped his bat and ran down the first base line, removing his batting gloves and sticking them into his pocket as he did so. He shot a glance at the stands, eager to see the proud faces of Mr. Baruth and Cheeko. But they were nowhere in sight.

The Redbirds surrounded him at the plate, jumping up and down as they exchanged high fives with him and with each other.

"Told you," Duane said, grinning.

Sylvester grinned back.

But that was it for the Redbirds that half inning. Neither Duane nor Bobby was able to continue the hitting streak.

Broton Tigers 3, Hooper Redbirds 5.

Josh Nichols led off for the Tigers in the top of the fourth. Short and squatty, he looked at Rick and waved the bat like a war club. Crack! A sharp hit over Jim Cowley's head for a single.

It was a good start. Jim Smith lashed out another single, advancing Josh all the way around to third. Then Chuck Manning came up and cleared the bases with a triple, tying up the score.

"Oh, no!" Sylvester moaned. Peering over at Chuck on third base, he could just see his grandslam home run going down the drain.

But none of the next three Tigers was able to do anything to bring the runner home. The inning ended with the score still tied, 5–5.

Sylvester trotted off the field, reached the dugout, and settled down. Again, there was a chance he might come up to bat. He couldn't imagine what might happen, but he didn't feel those strange flutterings in his stomach anymore. In fact, he was pretty sure he could handle things no matter what crossed the plate when it was his turn at bat. After all, he had come through last time — and without any "extra help."

It was a quick half inning as the Redbirds failed to put a single man on base. The Tigers came off the field with no traces of exertion.

Their leadoff batter, Lennie Chang, flied out to left field. That brought up B. K. Abbot, who doubled to right center.

Another out, and then an error by Duane, created a good scoring situation for the Tigers as Jim Smith, with two hits already to his credit, came up to the plate.

But Jim laced a grounder to second, resulting in the third out, and the Redbirds came off the field to start the bottom of the fifth inning.

Second baseman Jim Cowley walked on four pitches. It looked as though the Tigers' pitcher was a little tired after just batting and trying to beat out the throw to first. He didn't seem able to get one over.

That changed when Ted Sobel came to bat. The first pitch was straight over the heart of the plate. Ted walloped it into right center for a double. Coach Corbin arm-spun Jim in to home as Chuck Manning pegged in the ball. Jim barely made it as he hit the dirt and slid safely across the plate. Tigers 5, Redbirds 6.

Trent was up next. Sylvester put on his helmet, picked up his bat, and knelt in the on-deck circle. With only one out, there was no doubt he'd come up to bat again. But the old pressure, the question of whether it would be a home run or nothing, no longer mattered. He was comfortable with the fact that doing his best was all anyone could ask of him.

"Syl! You're up!" a voice shouted. It was Billy Haywood.

He hadn't even noticed what happened at the plate: Trent had just struck out in three straight pitches.

He jumped to his feet and passed Trent, who was walking back to the dugout with a disgusted look on his face.

"That's okay, Trent," Sylvester said without any sarcasm. "Can't do it all the time. You'll get 'em back."

Just for a second, Trent glanced at him, as if surprised to hear a kind word from Sylvester. But he continued, silently, toward the dugout.

Sylvester observed that Ted was still on second. He stepped to the plate and focused on the pitcher's mound. He got ready for the first pitch.

"Strike!" Jim Smith's curve ball just grazed the outside corner of the plate.

The next pitch was in there, and Sylvester swung. Crack! A long high drive to center field! It looked good!

The Redbirds' fans sprang to their feet, cheering and applauding, as Sylvester dropped his bat and headed for first base.

He ran slowly as he watched the soaring ball reach

its apex and start arcing down. From just the corner of his eye, he saw that Chuck Manning had his back close to the center field fence, his glove hand held high in the air.

A moment later the applause changed to sighs and moans of disappointment. The ball descended *not* on the other side of the fence, but into Chuck Manning's waiting glove.

17

For one second, Sylvester wanted to crawl under the turf and just disappear. But then, he shrugged off the feeling. At least he had given it his best shot. He lifted his head and started to run back toward the dugout.

And then the strangest thing of all happened. A cheer started in the stands. He could have sworn it was that squeaky, pesky voice of Snooky Malone's that he heard first.

"Coddmyer! Coddmyer! Coddmyer!"

It was picked up by a few others, then some more, then more, until a huge crowd was shouting his name all at once and clapping rhythmically.

It lasted less than a minute, but it was something he never forgot. Even though he hadn't hit a home run, hadn't even gotten a hit, the fans were still on his side. They appreciated what he had done. They hadn't forgotten.

Even the guys in the dugout were on their feet.

Rick: "It was real close. Too bad, Syl."

Eddie: "Couldn't get any closer without going over. Tough luck, Syl."

Jerry Ash: "Bum break, pal. You'll get 'em next time."

Sylvester was so flustered, he was at a loss for words. "Let's just hold them," he managed to sputter.

Good news came for his pal Duane, who was at bat. He hit a clean single to short right, scoring Ted. Bobby then grounded to retire the side. Three out. Tigers 5, Redbirds 7.

Chuck Manning led off with a walk to start the top of the sixth inning. "Oink" advanced him to third with a single, his first hit of the game. And then Rick walked Steve Cranshaw to load the bases.

Rats, thought Sylvester. The bases loaded, no outs, and their best hitter is up. So far, Mike Hennesey, the Tigers' cleanup hitter, had walked and gone down twice. He was still a threat that couldn't be underestimated.

He popped up to third and Duane snagged it. One out.

Lennie Chang swung at and missed three in a row. Two outs.

And then, B. K. Abbot stepped up to the plate, looking really strong. With his reputation as a long-ball hitter, the outfield backed up a few steps.

On Rick's first pitch, he blasted a fly that was just short of right center field. But it was a judgment call whether it was Bobby's or Sylvester's ball. It would be a hard catch for either of them, and both had to go for it.

The two outfielders raced in that direction, neither sure who would shout first, or whether they would collide in the attempt.

As time and space grew short, amid the uproar from the stands, a voice on the field cried, "Sylvester, it's yours! Go for it, buddy!"

It was Trent!

Bobby swerved out of the way and Sylvester made a horizontal leap that would have ended in a belly flop if he were diving into a swimming pool. But his glove was turned in the right direction, and he grabbed the ball in the webbing just before it touched down.

The game was over. The Redbirds won, 7–5, and Sylvester started to run off the field to the sound of the cheers and applause that rang from the stands. Before he could get as far as the infield, he was swept up by his teammates. Trent threw an arm around his shoulders and gave him a friendly punch. "Way to go, slugger," he said, and his smile was genuine.

The swarm of fans pouring down from the stands surrounded him, but he was able to pull away to spend a few minutes with the special people in his life before boarding the bus. His mother and father could hardly speak, they were so hoarse from shouting.

"We're definitely going out to dinner tonight," his mother croaked.

"Yes." His father agreed. "And you get to pick the restaurant."

Sylvester grabbed someone standing near him and winked at the girl hovering a few steps away.

"Okay, but can I bring a couple of friends? I'd like Snooky and Joyce to come," he said.

His father laughed. "The more the merrier!"

"Okay, then, one more," he said as his eyes scanned the crowd. "If he hasn't disappeared, I'd like to ask him to join us."

"Him? Who?" Mrs. Coddmyer asked.

"Mr. Baruth," said Sylvester. "I guess he's gone. I wonder if I'll ever see him again."

Snooky piped up, "According to your stars, you're still in for a few surprises, Sylvester."

Sylvester threw up his arms, shook his head, and boarded the bus.

MATT CHRISTOPHER

The #1 Sports Writer for Kids

Read them all!

All available in paperback from Little, Brown and Company

Matt Christopher

Sports Bio Bookshelf

Andre Agassi

John Elway

Wayne Gretzky

Ken Griffey Jr.

Mia Hamm

Grant Hill

Randy Johnson

Michael Jordan

Lisa Leslie

Tara Lipinski

Greg Maddux

Hakeem Olajuwon

Emmitt Smith

Mo Vaughn

Tiger Woods

Steve Young